A Letter from Brandi Chastain

Hi Again Everyone!

I hope you are as excited as I am for the new *Soccer Sisters* book!

Being a part of a team, any team, is one of the greatest experiences you can have. You win together and you lose together, but mostly you learn and grow together.

Being on a team forges a special kind of understanding and togetherness that can push you forward. It creates a sisterhood of friendships that you just can't find in many other ways.

I was proud to be a part of the United States Women's National Team for the exciting 1999 World Cup, and am often asked what my favorite moment from that tournament was. Most people would assume that it was when I had the chance to kick the game-winning penalty kick, but they would probably be surprised by the correct answer.

My best moment looked like my worst moment.

Early in the quarterfinal game against Germany, I scored an "own goal," against our team. Suddenly, we were losing and it was my fault. But, before I had time to have a negative thought about myself or the possible outcome of the game, our great captain, Carla Overbeck, was there to talk to me. Right away she said, "don't worry about it," and reminded me that there was still lots of game to play and that we were going to get that goal back and win. And we did.

I never thought making such a big mistake would change my life in such a positive way.

In that moment, my teammate made me understand that she still had my back. She made me see that I didn't have to be perfect. She allowed me to feel the trust and vulnerability among soccer sisters. Because she was there for me, instead of the worst moment of the tournament, it was empowering, and in the end, the most impactful.

These are the kinds of lessons you can learn on the field and in the *Soccer Sisters* series. Vee, Lily, and all the Bombers have their highs and lows, but through it all, they always have each other.

Keep reading and kicking!

Brandi Chastain

Praise for *Soccer Sisters: Lily Out of Bounds*

Napa County Reads 2012 Official Selection

"As a mom of two daughters I'm always looking for books about strong girls and sports and all the good things that can trickle down from being part of a team. This one hit the mark on all those levels. Highly recommend." —Jenny Rosenstrach, *Dinner: A Love Story*

"The *Soccer Sisters* series isn't just about soccer. It's about friendships, family and the awesome thrill that comes from winning. It's also fun, which is the best reason in the world to read it." —Carl Hiaasen

"Anyone with a daughter should have this book. The soccer sisters' team code is really a code for life. My favorite was beating the boys at recess. Way to go Lily, as my daughter would say, you rock!" —Ray Leone, Head Coach of Women's Soccer, Harvard University

Praise for *Breakaway*
by Andrea Montalbano

"A winning book by a talented newcomer." —Mike Lupica

"Montalbano's love of the game is evident in the detailed, technical description of each play. Her description of youth sports tackles fanatical fans, overbearing parents, and jealous peers." —Kirkus Reviews

"It's an ideal pick for readers more interested in scoring goals than boyfriends" —Publishers Weekly

Soccer Sisters

Book 2

Vee: Caught Offside

Andrea Montalbano

In This Together Media

New York, New York

In This Together Media
New York

In This Together Media Edition, July 2013

Copyright @ 2013 by Andrea Montalbano

Published in the United States by In This Together Media, New York, 2013

www.inthistogethermedia.com

BISAC: Soccer (Sports & Recreation) – Juvenile Fiction. 2. Girls and Women – Juvenile Fiction. 3. Friendship (social issues) – Juvenile Fiction. 4. Hispanic and Latino (United States – People and Places) – Juvenile Fiction.

ISBN: 978-0-9898956-8-6

eBook ISBN: 978-0-9858956-9-3

Cover Design and Photo: Evan Rich
Evanrphotography.com

Interior and Ebook Design: Steven W. Booth
GeniusBookServices.com

For all my Soccer Sisters!

Chapter 1.

It's not always easy to fit in, especially when you're a kid.

When you're little, it's simple. Conquer the basics: tie your shoes, ride a bike, learn to read, make some friends.

Easy. After a few knots and tumbles, most kids figure it out.

But by the time she hit double digits, Vee Merino figured out that life gets way more complicated. Now, she faced not only the tests her teachers hand out but also the real-life pop quizzes of navigating modern middle school existence.

Halls overflowed with cliques, clubs, hormones, and peer pressure.

Talk about angst overload.

Unless, like Vee, you were a Soccer Sister. Being a part of the Brookville Bombers U13 travel team was like having a protective social shield. Every time Vee slipped her blue and yellow uniform over her head and felt her jersey number slide down her back, she felt part of something wonderful, real, and legit.

Her team.

Pitfalls and social anxiety fell away, and all of a sudden the chaos of life appeared clean, simple, and organized. School was for studying; a boy was just someone who might also want to kick around; friends were always waiting with cleats on and balls ready to roll.

Getting to winter practice on time, however, was often a true challenge.

"Are we late again?" a voice asked from the backseat. It was Vee's BFF, teammate, cohort of every level, #7 on the Bombers, center-midfielder, sometimes temperamental, but overall fan favorite, Lily James, aka, LJ. Vee looked at the car clock then turned to answer.

"Believe it or not, only like two minutes," she said. "Might be a record!"

Lily gave a small cheer, gathered up her ball and water bottle, and zipped up her jacket. Vee loved that her buddy was born ready for action.

"Brrr, it's freezing," Lily said, exhaling a puff of vapor. Even in the small car, the temperature was chilling. Vee and Lily lived in neighboring suburbs just north of New York City. It was mid-February and Old Man Winter was still working hard. No early retirement for him.

"You know it's not much warmer inside the Dome," Vee commented, nodding toward the enormous white indoor soccer facility.

The girls shivered in unison. The only winter soccer facility near Brookville was pretty much nothing more than a turf field covered by a giant, dirty, inflated tent. It looked like half of a massive, grimy golf ball sticking out of the ground. Inside there was no heat, except the kind made by running and kicking.

"*Papi*, just let us out here, *por favor*," Vee asked her father, Tomas, in a mix of English and Spanish.

"*Si, pero m'ija*, where are your sweat pants?" Tomas asked with a heavy accent. He motioned towards Vee's outfit. Wearing only a sweatshirt, jacket, and soccer shorts, her legs were bare at the knees. Nubby goose bumps covered the entire middle section of Vee's legs.

"Oh, I forgot them. It's fine *Papi,* we will be running the whole time," Vee answered quickly.

Tomas' face registered concern. The wind howled, shaking the car slightly. Vee thought the weather was conspiring with her father.

"Look," Vee said. "I'll just pull my socks up over my knees and pull my shorts down low and there will only be a tiny strip of skin showing."

Vee yanked at her white tube sock, stretching the nylon fabric up over her knee.

"See?" She said to her father, trying to get the furrow of worry from his brow to release. Tomas seemed to relax momentarily, until a horrible ripping sound filled the tiny car.

"*Aye!*" Tomas yelled.

"Oh, dude," Vee muttered to herself. Looking down, she could feel and see the giant hole she'd torn in her tube sock.

"What the heck was that?" Lily asked, peering into the front seat.

"I totally trashed my sock," Vee held up her leg to show the damage. A tear, about six inches across, exposed the back of her right calf. Vee looked at the threadbare fabric. Man, those socks were really old.

Lily started to laugh and Tomas rolled his eyes.

"Do you have another sock?" Lily asked.

Vee shook her head. "Who carries three socks around?"

"Another pair of socks!" Lily yelled with a laugh.

Vee looked at the clock again. She had to think fast. Searching her soccer bag, she found nothing but a half-eaten snack bar and an empty water bottle.

"*Mi amor*, you cannot go to practice like that," Tomas said firmly.

"Oh man, we are so late now. Coach Chris is going to make us do like a million push ups," Lily said. She looked at Vee's leg. "What are you going to do? Your sock is hanging on … uh, literally, by a thread."

Vee expanded her search to her father's car. She fumbled under her seat and pulled out a pile of papers and an old pair of shorts.

"*Papi*, this is why it's so cold in your car! Look!" Vee showed her father the crack in the floor of the old sedan. Icy air was flowing in like a raging river.

"*Donde*?" Tomas asked.

"*Aquí*, look," Vee said. The car is old and in bad shape, Vee thought. Just another something new they can't afford. She shrugged and watched as Tomas felt under the seat. His eyes opened wide when he felt the cold air hit his fingers. As if on cue, another gust of wind whipped through the little car.

"Oh, look! This is perfect!" Vee exclaimed, emerging from under the driver's seat with a small piece of fabric that looked like something from the U.S. Army.

"What is that?" Lily asked.

"It's a bandana," Vee said. "Watch this." She took the camouflaged square and folded it into a triangle, then folded it again into a long strip. Quickly, she wrapped the bandana around the hole in her leg, folded the torn sock over the top, and tucked the ends inside. The result was a white sock with a trendy camo trim.

"Okay, I don't know how you did that," Lily said, her head titled slightly. "But, that's actually pretty cool!"

"And it better keep you warm," Tomas added.

"Let's go!" Vee exclaimed and the two giggling girls scrambled out of the car. A jumble of bags, balls and jackets rolled into the dark, icy parking lot.

"I'll see you two *locas* at the restaurant," Tomas said with a chuckle.

"Yes, Tabitha's driving us, and, remember, she's staying for dinner," Vee reminded her father excitedly. The trio, LJ, Vee, and Tabitha, had started a new after-practice dinner tradition: dinner at *Katerina's. Katerina's* was the name of the restaurant owned by Lily's father. It was in Brookville, where Lily and most of the Bombers lived. For as long as Vee could remember, Tomas had been the restaurant's manager.

Tomas nodded and waved as he pulled away. The two girls hurried toward the entrance. The girls held onto each other as their flat indoor shoes provided no traction on the super-dangerous patches of black ice.

"Hey, wait up!" they heard a voice cry. It was their teammate Olivia. She trudged up behind Lily and Vee.

"Hey Olivia," Vee said, slowing down to wait for

her teammate. Olivia was one of the biggest girls on the team and a really strong defender. She had brown hair and oddly dark eyebrows. "That parking lot is a mess. My mom had to drop me way back there," Olivia said, gesturing behind her. Turning her head, she noticed Tomas' car. "Jeez, Vee, nice ride. What a clunker."

Vee laughed and answered, "I know, but my father loves that old wreck for some reason."

"Let's gooo already!" Lily chided, "I'm turning into a popsicle." The three girls pushed their way through the revolving door and into the soccer dome.

Vee shivered when she got inside, "Oh, dude, it's just as cold in here!"

Lily and Olivia nodded in chilly agreement.

"Well, at least there isn't any wind," Lily said, and all three girls looked up to the dome's ceiling just as an icy gust made the lights sway in unison.

"Yikes," said Olivia.

"I've never seen the lights move like that before," Lily observed.

"It's fine," Vee said. "Let's go."

Vee scanned the fields for her team.

"There they are," Olivia said.

Vee spied the Bombers gathered on the far side and noticed immediately that they had missed warm up completely. They were gathered around their long-time coach, Chris Moore, who was already in the middle of explaining the first drill. Avery, Reese, and Beth all shared annoyed looks on their faces.

"Uh oh," Vee muttered. "Dude, I'm sorry to make you so late again."

LJ just smiled and shrugged.

"Hey, Vee, what's that on your leg?" Olivia asked as the girls jogged over to meet their team.

"Oh, nothing," Vee answered as she and Lily shared a sly smile.

"Oh, nice of you girls to join us," Chris said, holding up his hand to stop them from coming any closer. "That's two full laps and 20 push ups. All three of you. Get going. Practice is at six o'clock, not six-oh-eight."

Vee, Lily, and Olivia sighed together, then turned away from the group of girls and started their run around the field.

"Sorry, LJ," Vee said again.

"Oh, forget about it already. It's no biggie!" LJ answered. "Let's go. At least we can get warm!"

"Oh man, I hate running laps and I hate push ups more," Olivia complained as soon as they rounded the first corner. "My stupid father couldn't find his keys. It's not my fault I was late."

"Well, it doesn't bother me," Lily answered. "I just don't want to miss too many of the drills. Plus, I'm cold, and you know how Chris can talk."

Vee nodded in agreement. Coach Chris was sort of a strategist, psychologist, and a surfer dude all mixed up in one. He often made the girls suffer through his long talks and "Think Time." Vee knew being this late was a surefire way to get a speech about commitment.

Lily picked up the pace. "Let's go!"

Vee smiled at her soccer-obsessed best friend. There was nothing about soccer that Lily didn't love. Even running a lap because they were late. Even Think Time. And there was pretty much nothing about Lily that Vee didn't love. They were just a perfect pair. Physically, the two girls could not have looked more different. Lily was tall and Vee was tiny. Lily was fair with Irish freckles and bright eyes that were a mix of green, blue, and yellow. Vee was from Mexico. Her skin was like cocoa. Her hair was so black that in some lights it looked blue, and her big, brown eyes were steady and warm. The two girls had been friends since they were babies. Lily's mom used to say they were "buddies in buckets." Buckets being the baby car seats with a handle that looked, well, like buckets. Vee and Lily had learned to love soccer together, playing behind *Katerina's* from the time they could toddle. The busboys and waiters, most of them Hispanic, adored the little girls who loved *fútbol*. They were never without teammates. Anyone on break was ready to play with the two tiny and adorable soccer nuts.

Vee kept pace with Lily and Olivia, but she was jogging just a few steps behind them, warming up slowly. She could hear the howl of the wind outside and feel the cold rush from the ventilation cracks in the dome's lining. Vee was drawn to the line of lights hanging from the ceiling; she noticed that each was contained in a metal cage so that when (not if) it got hit with a ball, no glass shattered down on the players. Someone had to have thought of that, Vee mused. She really liked to observe people and things. She didn't let on, not even to Tomas or Lily, but Vee spent a lot of her life watching and trying to figure out what made people tick.

"Look at the lights," Vee said, intrigued.

Lily looked up, "It's like a creepy, cold disco in here tonight."

"Speaking of disco," Olivia said. "LJ, do you know who you are going to ask to the dance?"

"No clue," Lily answered while rounding the last corner. "Haven't thought about it, and still trying to get out of it."

"Dance?" Vee had no idea what they were talking about.

"Oh, this dumb Brookville thing, 'The Snow Fairy Dance,'" Lily answered. "My mom is making me go."

"I am soo excited," Olivia said. "Because the best

part is that the girls get to ask the boys and the boys have to say yes to the first girl who invites them."

"Best part?" Lily asked. "Try nightmare. All the girls are freaking out about which boy to invite. It's bad enough to have to be asked, it's worse to have to be the ask-er."

"What do you mean has to say 'yes'? Boys can't ask girls to the dance?" Vee was confused.

Olivia jumped right in. "Right. If a girl asks a boy who isn't already going to the dance he has to say yes! I think it's genius."

Vee thought it didn't sound that great to her. If you are girl, you have to do the asking. If you are a boy, not only can you not ask a girl if you want to, but you have to say yes to any girl who asks, even if they are totally annoying. Vee had yet to find her first crush. Instead of feeling left out, she felt grateful all this dance nonsense was going on in Brookville.

"Well, I already know who I'm asking," Olivia boasted. "And I've got to do it right away because he is so popular, I know he'll be picked right up."

"Who?" Vee asked, only slightly curious.

"Oh, right. Like I'm going to tell anyone!" Olivia responded.

Vee was taken aback by Olivia's sharp response and regretted her question. "Whatever, dude," she replied defensively, "I don't even live in Brookville or go to your school."

Vee attended middle school in Highland Ferry. Tomas, and lots of other folks who lived in Highland Ferry, worked for people in Brookville. Brookville was mostly large homes, restaurants, and pricey boutiques. Vee's middle school didn't offer a soccer team for girls, nor did her town, which was why she started playing on the Brookville squad. That, and she and Lily were inseparable.

Vee sprinted ahead of Olivia for the final leg of the warm-up run and plopped down close to the rest of the team to stretch. There were only nine girls at practice because the winter season was optional, so the team was smaller. They played games with seven players on each side, instead of eleven. The fields were also smaller, but the tighter spaces suited Vee's game perfectly. She was a striker and had a reputation for her amazing speed and dribbling abilities. Even though she was smaller than most of the rest of the team and twelve, young for her grade, that didn't matter at all in indoor soccer. It was skill and quick thinking that made Vee stand out even more than she did during the outdoor season.

Vee started on her push-ups as Lily and Olivia caught up. She watched Olivia finish her last lap with

Lily and wondered why she was acting weird about a dance. To Vee, the whole concept of crushes, boys, and dances seemed like a vague and dreary task waiting somewhere far off on the horizon. Vee was much more interested in soccer.

"All the way down, girls!" a voice teased. Vee looked up from her second push-up to see Tabitha Gordon, hands on hips, standing over her. Tabitha smiled at Vee and offered her hand when she was finally done with her last late-for-practice push up.

"I'm so glad you're here," Tabitha said. "All these girls have gone completely nuts."

"Because we are late?" Vee answered with a question, feeling worried that her team was angry with her.

Tabitha laughed. "No, because of this dumb dance. It's non-stop negotiation. I can't understand why they are so worked up. It's annoying."

"Oh, no. All of them? Olivia already wigged out on me about it." Vee glanced at the rest of her team, who were deep in conversation, hardly paying attention to the passing drill Chris had set up for them. Tabitha rolled her eyes and Vee smiled. She knew her friend would never let anything social concern her. Tabitha Gordon was by far the most popular girl in Brookville. For starters, she was gorgeous. She had the straightest, longest, most perfect platinum hair. Her flow-y locks could inspire Taylor Swift to write a chart-topping revenge song. She'd been a ballet dancer since she was three and had so far sachayed her way around the whole awkward tween phase. The Gordons also lived in the biggest and fanciest house in Brookville. Vee was one of the few people who knew Tabitha's life wasn't perfect, but when it came to something like a dance, her buddy had it covered.

"Hey Tabitha!" Olivia said, arriving with Lily. They started their push-ups.

"Hey Olivia. Hey LJ," Tabitha said. "How's the jog?"

Lily smiled. "Well, I'm not freezing anymore!"

"Okay, Chris told me to tell you the drill." Vee could see Chris setting up cones on the far side of the field. "We're doing three versus two. You, me, and Vee are starting on offense. Olivia, you're on defense, over there with Avery."

"Dude! I love 3v2's!" Vee said. She also loved the word "dude." With the right tone and attitude, Vee knew "dude" could convey nearly any emotion. Right now, she was psyched because 3v2's were her specialty. Three offensive players started at midfield and tried to score on two defenders and a goalie. Because they out-numbered the defenders by one player, the offense was expected to get a shot off every single time. The key, Vee knew, was that very first pass.

Chris blew his whistle, and Vee started off with the ball on the right side. Tabitha was on the left and Lily was in her spot in the middle. She quickly tapped the ball with her left foot and dribbled sharply at Avery, the defender on her side. The trick was to draw Avery to her by moving toward the goal quickly. The defender had no choice but to try and take the ball, or Vee would be in a position to just go straight to goal and shoot.

Avery approached, crouching low, and then back-pedaled, shadowing Vee like Spider Man as she pushed toward the goal. She watched Vee's feet carefully, looking for an opening to steal the ball, but also trying to slow her down and herd her to the outside of the field. Some players made the mistake of stabbing at the ball with their foot, getting off balance and making it easy for an offender like Vee to slip past and get a cross off to the middle of the field. But Avery was an experienced defender, and she didn't rush.

Vee dribbled, keeping her eyes up and ears open.

"Through ball!" she heard a voice yell and saw that Lily was making her move—a diagonal run toward the goal. Olivia was slow to respond, and Lily broke free. Vee passed the ball on the outside of Avery and Lily collected it easily. Then Vee made her run. In soccer, you have to pass and move. You never just observe the action. Ball watching was a sin on the Bombers. Lily crossed the ball to Tabitha, who was wide open in front of the net. Tabitha laid it off to Vee, who was flying in and fired off a screamer.

The goalie, Beth, had no chance as the ball slammed into the back of the net.

Vee, Lily, and Tabitha hi-fived in the middle of the field and then started jogging back to half field.

"Stop!" Coach Chris bellowed. The girls slowed. "Everyone freeze. Vee, LJ, and Tabitha, get back into the original formation. Olivia and Avery, you too."

The girls shared a look. This wasn't good.

Chris grabbed the ball and passed it back to Vee.

"Okay, Vee, now in half-speed, dribble down the line again." Vee sprinted back into place and did as she was told, repeating the same path but much more slowly.

Chris continued, "Okay, now Avery, you did a good job of slowing Vee down. Lily, you made an excellent run to the line. Olivia? Where did you make your mistake?"

Olivia shrugged her shoulders and looked at the ground, mumbling "Dunno."

"You let Lily get ball-side of you, and instead of following her on her run, you were just watching and not really covering anybody."

Olivia shoulders sagged and she looked at the ground.

"Okay, now LJ, make that run again," Chris said, guiding Olivia gently by the arm. "Olivia, now you stay with her, always keeping yourself between the goal and the player, in this case, LJ. Try it again, girls, but this time, Tabitha, you start with the ball."

The next few runs went much more smoothly and before Vee knew it Chris called for a water break. As she jogged over to the sidelines, Vee felt a rush of cold air hit her calf.

"Here." Tabitha ran up to Vee and handed her the camouflage bandana.

"Oh, thanks," Vee said, grateful to be able to cover up. "I'm getting goose bumps already!"

"Hey Vee, can't you afford a whole sock?" Olivia said, in a joking voice.

Vee picked up the bandana and retied it over the hole in her sock. "I guess I better get some new ones."

"Seriously. And while you're at it, a new ride." Olivia was laughing as she said this, but Vee heard a strange edge to her voice. "Your car is a hunk o' junk."

"Well, I think the bandana is pretty cool," Tabitha said. "Maybe I'll wear one next practice."

Vee flashed Tabitha a smile of gratitude and again felt surprised at Olivia. She began to wonder if maybe Olivia was mad at her? Vee tried to recall anything she might have said or done to anger her teammate. Vee had scored every time she got the ball during the last drill, but that was pretty normal. Vee was about to ask her if everything was all right when a huge gust of wind blew open one of the dome's front doors. A blast of icy air rushed onto the field and the girls shrieked their disapproval and fear. One of the coaches rushed to secure the flapping door. The dome took on an eerie feel, as everyone stopped playing. It was oddly quiet, except for the howling wind. The kids on the fields looked up because the lights were swaying precariously over their heads.

Immediately, whistles blew as coaches gathered their teams.

"Bombers! Over here!" Chris called. "Get out from under that light!"

The glass might not break, but all the lights looked to Vee like they might come crashing down. Two other coaches continued to struggle with the door. Every time it seemed they had secured the revolving panes, another arctic blast would rip through, making a terrible crashing noise as one door slammed against the other. No one could come in or go out the main entrance. The swinging lights cast crazy shadows on the sides of the dome and the temperature started to plummet. Vee and the rest of the Bombers huddled together wondering what was coming next.

It wasn't long before the power flickered off and on, and then off again, leaving the Sports Dome totally, utterly dark.

"Oh, I don't like this," LJ shivered.

The lights came back on quickly, but the door continued to slam and then the entire dome itself seemed to be heaving against the violent winter squalls.

"Okay, I really don't like this," LJ repeated, grabbing Vee by the arm.

"Girls, let's start moving toward that emergency exit," Chris said, pointing to a door across the field. "Stay together."

The Bombers moved to gather their bags and balls when the lights flickered again.

"Just get your jackets if they are close and follow me. Everyone hold hands," Chris instructed. All of the girls grabbed hands and arms. Chris latched on to Vee's arm to lead them and said, "Stick close."

"I dropped my ball," Avery cried. Her pink and neon orange soccer ball rolled across the turf.

"Leave it," Chris ordered. Vee could feel the tension in his grip and hear the stress in his voice.

The Bombers moved like a shuffling train, arms linked, toward the exit. Vee had Chris on one side and Lily on the other. Lily was squeezing Vee's upper arm like a vice. Another howl of the wind seemed to shift the entire ceiling and, for the first time, Vee was a little frightened too. The Bombers picked up the pace to a trot, the neon pink EXIT sign beckoning their escape.

With just twenty feet to go, the power cut for good. Vee and the rest of the team were engulfed by blackness. Only the Exit sign shone dimly ahead. Vee looked up, but the top of the dome was as black as the ground in front of her.

Vee leaned on LJ and whispered, "Dude."

Chapter 2.

"Okay girls, we're going to keep moving toward that sign and gather outside. It's going to be really cold. Try and get your coats on and stick together as soon as we get out."

"If we get out..." Beth said in a nervous voice.

"Of course we're getting out," Vee said calmly. "The door is right there."

The team shuffled forward, arms entwined. Chris found the door handle with an outstretched arm, and let go of Vee. She could hear him grunting to try and get the door open against the howling wind.

"Vee, LJ, help me," Chris commanded.

The two girls moved forward and used the weight of their bodies to shove the door with their shoulders. Vee was nearly a head shorter than Lily and probably about fifteen pounds lighter. She was also nine months younger than Lily and had always been small for her age. Still, she was tough, wiry, and strong. Mostly, she was determined. She had grit.

"On three," Chris said, "One…Two…Three!"

Vee leaned against the door and pushed with all her might. She used her legs. She grunted. Finally, the door cracked slightly and a blast of wind hit her right in the face. It startled her and she tried to catch her breath. The door slammed back shut.

"Again," Chris said. "Girls, help us."

"We can do it!" Vee yelled. "Come on!"

More of the Bombers gathered behind Chris, Vee, and Lily and they all pushed together. Suddenly, the wind caught the metal door and slammed it all the way open with an alarming and violent crash. The team jumped and screamed.

Vee wanted to get out of the dome, but outside wasn't much better. The wind was whipping past with a creepy howl. The immediate area behind the dome was pitch black, too. The only light was from a building in the distance.

"Whoa. The whole area must be out of power," Tabitha said from behind them.

"Okay, let's go. Everyone out," Chris said. "I know it's cold, but we can't stay in here. It's too dangerous. If you have a jacket get it on. Keep your fingers in your pockets and we'll head toward the parking lot and get into the cars."

Vee and the Bombers shuffled into the cold blackness.

"Maybe living in California would be nice," Lily joked.

"Or Florida," Avery chimed in with a shiver. "I never thought I'd say this, but I'd be happy to move in with my grandparents."

"Or Hawaii!" added Beth. "We can start a surf team! Called the Bubblers."

"Anywhere but this frozen popsicle stand!" Lily yelled.

Vee loved that her team could kid around at a time like this. As a group, they had been through muddy losses and sunny wins, and Vee knew that adversity always brought them closer together. Plus, they were a giggly crew.

Chris shuttled the girls forward, counting heads as they exited the doomed dome. Soon, they were stumbling on rocks and roots in the wooded area that led back to the parking lot. Like a welcoming North Star, a small beam of light illuminated the path ahead. Vee looked behind her to see where the light was coming from. Tabitha was holding up her cell phone.

She shrugged and smiled, "Flashlight app. Never leave home without it."

Vee cracked a smile and thought, leave it to Tabitha to have the latest gear. Arms linked, the girls moved *en masse* to the parking lot in front of the Dome. A group of frightened parents had gathered at the main entrance unable to get inside because the entrance door was still unsecured. They rushed forward to gather their kids.

Avery's mother, Mrs. Dwyer, and Olivia's father were the first Bomber parents to reach the team.

"Are you girls alright?" Mrs. Dwyer asked the team. "The whole far side of the dome looks like it's about to collapse!"

"I can take some of you home," Chris offered. Most of the parents had just dropped the girls off. It would be a few minutes before they came back to pick them up. Vee wondered how she, LJ, and Tabitha would get to the restaurant. She would be mortified to have to have her father drive anyone other than Lily. She rubbed her icy knees in the cold and pulled her jacket tighter, suddenly wishing she had listened to her father and worn sweatpants after all.

"Tabitha, do you want a ride home with me?" Olivia asked.

"Oh thanks, Olivia, but Rini is on his way. I texted him already," Tabitha replied casually. "LJ and Vee are coming with me, coach."

"Okay girls, I'll be in touch about this weekend," Chris said, watching as one by one the girls' parents arrived to get them out of the cold. "Game is home this weekend, so I'll have to work on getting us a new location or we'll have no choice but to forfeit."

The Bombers shrieked in horror. Forfeiting was not in their vocabulary. There were only two games left in the indoor season, and they were heading for a showdown for their first-ever indoor title. A forfeit would throw that all away. Vee sneered at the sky. She was sick of winter.

"I'll find a field," Chris tried to reassure them.

"Tabitha, are you sure you don't need a ride?" Olivia asked again. "We can take you home if you don't want to wait. It's really cold out here."

"Yeah, I'm sure, but thanks. Rini will be here soon." Rini, Vee knew, was the man who drove Tabitha around when her parents couldn't. The first time Vee heard Tabitha's family had a driver, she thought she was living in some kind of Disney movie. No one in her world had anything like that. Lots of people she knew in Highland Ferry didn't even have a car. But Tabitha's mom and dad both worked constantly and Tabitha and her brother had so many after school activities, they hired Rini to drive them wherever they needed to go.

"Are you sure? It's really cold out here," Olivia asked one more time.

Tabitha looked surprised that Olivia wouldn't let it go.

"I'm good," Tabitha said firmly.

Even in the darkness, Vee saw a look of consternation flush over Olivia's face. She smiled at Olivia, trying to ease the awkwardness in the air. Instead of returning the smile, Olivia's scowl deepened and she picked up her bag.

Then she turned on her heel and stormed off without another word.

Chapter 3.

"I didn't fhtink fhis was a methican resthruant!" Tabitha said, or tried to, as spicy green tomatillo sauce dribbled down her chin.

Vee and Lily stared slacked-jawed at their dainty friend as she shoveled another bite of shrimp taco into her already stuffed mouth. Tabitha closed her eyes as if their dinner was transporting her to a happy place. Head thrown back, chewing and smiling all at once, she was completely unaware that her face was a total mess and her cheeks were stuffed like a gorged hamster.

If only Taylor Swift could see her now.

Vee tried not to laugh, but had truly never imagined such a sight. She and Lily were used to their fathers' amazing meals, but apparently Tabitha and good food were just getting to know one another. Vee was still amazed that she and Tabitha had become such close friends. When Tabitha first joined the team they were U10's, and she was standoffish with a reputation of being a total snob. It had taken Vee and Lily that first season to realize that while she might be the Queen Bee at her school, at home she was under constant pressure from her parents. Tabitha had initially lacked the confidence to really give soccer her full one hundred percent. Her father wanted her to pursue a ballet career. Vee had learned a lot by watching Tabitha stand up to her family to get to stay on the team.

"That. Is. So. Beyond. Amazthing." Tabitha announced, finally taking a break. "What is in there?"

"I'm pretty sure it's shrimp, avocados, salsa, a little queso fresco and a squeeze of lime," Vee answered with a casual shrug.

"Okay, that is crazy delicious. Maybe the best thing I have ever eaten in my life."

"I'm glad you like it!" Lily said. "Tell my dad. Maybe he will finally listen to us and let Tomas put some non-Italian items on the menu."

Vee nodded. "We've been bugging him for a while to add those tacos."

"Can we have that again next week?" Tabitha asked.

Lily made a face. "If there is practice next week. That was scary tonight."

Vee heard a noise and noticed the kitchen door inch open.

"*Cómo están mis* super stars?" Tomas asked, poking his head out from the kitchen to check on the girls.

The door opened and Lily's father Liam followed right behind.

"Oh, so happy happy happy," Tabitha answered immediately, patting her flat toned belly.

"Wait!" Tabitha thought for a moment and then said proudly, "*Muy contenta.*"

Tomas beamed. Tabitha and Tomas had made a deal. He would speak more English if she would practice more Spanish. Tomas knew how to speak English, but just felt more comfortable in Spanish. Tabitha only knew a little from having studied ballet in Spain the previous summer.

"And full?" Liam asked.

The girls nodded. Vee started to ask her father to make it again next week, but Tabitha beat her to it.

"Mr. Merino? That was the most amazing thing I have ever eaten in my entire existence on this planet. Even better than the lasagna we had last week. Can you please make it for us again? I can't wait!" Tabitha blurted out. Then added, "There was no way I could say all that in Spanish."

"*Por supuesto*! Of course!" Tomas answered, and Vee thought she saw her father stand a little taller. No one missed the smug glance he shot Lily's father, Liam. Lily and Vee both cracked up. Both girls enjoyed their fathers' constant sparring over recipes and who could make the most popular special of the week.

"*Muchas gracias*," Tabitha said.

Liam stroked the top of Lily's head. "Your mom called. Chris called and told her about the dome collapsing."

"Oh, no he didn't!" Lily cried. Vee and Tabitha looked at one another.

"Wait, what?" Vee asked. "Back up. It COLLAPSED? As in fell down? It was standing when we left."

Tomas put his hand to his mouth. Lily said what they were all thinking. "This is not good."

Lily's mother Toni was a well-established worrier. She was legendary for letting her imagination run wild, anticipating the worst possible outcome, and as a result, occasionally shutting down events that scared her. If Lily's mom thought the Dome had collapsed anywhere near her child, there was a good chance she'd ban winter soccer altogether.

"Yep. The dome, did, in fact, partially collapse," Liam said. "And yes, Lily, your mother has been informed. Luckily no one was inside and no one got hurt. It should be fixed and back up in a month or so."

Vee thought for a second. "A month!"

"Well, it will at least give me time to calm down my mom," Lily said, and Tabitha laughed.

But Vee felt a minor shot of panic course through her body. For her, being a part of the Bombers was more than just playing soccer. It made her whole life better. It made her life complete. Even these after-practice dinners meant so much to Vee. Since her father was the manager of *Katerina's*, she spent a lot of nights alone with the television, or in the back office of the restaurant. There were only two in her family. Vee's mother had died when she was just a baby, and she didn't have any brothers or sisters. Most of her extended family currently lived in Mexico, Texas, or Michigan, so she only saw them on holidays or in the summer. Vee couldn't even imagine how empty her life would be without her team.

"Where are we going to play? When are we going to get a field? What's going to happen?" Vee asked a series of rapid-fire questions in an ever-increasing voice of alarm.

"I have no idea," Liam told the girls. "Chris said he hasn't found a place for you yet."

"Well, what about the game this weekend?" Vee asked. "Did we have to forfeit?"

"He's working on it, he said. Take it easy girls." Liam urged, and he and Tomas retreated back to the kitchen.

Vee, Lily, and Tabitha tried to get going on their homework, but they were too distracted to get much done. After a few minutes Lily stretched and yawned. "So Tabitha, who are you inviting to this dance?"

Tabitha shrugged and Vee was happy to see that her friend seemed to have very little interest in the topic. She barely lifted her head.

"Ah, I dunno. Maybe that cute guy Will from Science class," she answered nonchalantly.

Lily's mouth hung open, "Tabitha, Will is like the best-looking kid, best athlete and most popular kid in the school! Him, and your brother, Mark, I guess."

Tabitha remained unimpressed. "Well, I'm definitely not asking my brother. And maybe I won't ask Will. I think I'd rather he ask me."

"What do you mean?" Vee asked. "Olivia told me the girls have to ask the boys and the boys have to say 'yes'."

"Olivia has a lot to learn," Tabitha smiled. "There are ways around this stuff. I might ask Will if I feel like it. But my brother gave me the scoop."

"Do tell!" Lily urged.

Tabitha lowered her voice and looked around, as if a horde of 7th and 8th graders were hidden behind the furniture. "Lots of guys make it clear they don't want to be asked because if they aren't asked then later they can invite whoever they want."

Vee was totally confused. "How can they control if a girl asked them or not? I don't get it. This whole thing is stupid and complicated. I wish it would just go away. Am I the only one worried that the Bombers are about to forfeit their first game ever?"

"If you're annoyed by the dance chat now," Tabitha laughed, "just wait!"

"Well, maybe LJ, you should invite G-4," Vee said with a snort. She knew mentioning G-4, a boy in town who Lily could not stand, would get a good reaction.

As if on cue, Lily made a noise that sounded like a cross between a snorting pig and a horse blowing a fly off its lips. Then, she pretended that she was throwing up. She put her hands to her neck as if she were choking and threw herself on the ground.

Vee laughed so hard she momentarily forgot her soccer woes.

"Actually," Tabitha said, "I think Olivia likes G-4."

"You have got to be kidding me," Lily said, getting up from the floor. "He is 100 percent unlikable."

Tabitha shrugged and said, "Lid for every pot."

Vee thought back to practice and Olivia's behavior. "Speaking of Olivia, did you guys notice she was being a little weird today?

"I didn't really notice anything," Lily said, shaking her head and pretending to do her Social Studies report.

Tabitha also answered, "Nope."

An odd pit of doubt swirled in Vee's stomach. She was certain something was bothering Olivia, certain that she had been acting sort of weird, and if she were honest with herself, mean. But, if no one else noticed it, maybe she was imagining it?

Vee sighed audibly and Lily looked back up from her homework.

"You okay?" Lily asked.

Vee started to tell her what was bothering her, but stopped when Tomas burst through the door armed with a tray with three flans, all topped with whipped cream.

Tabitha actually clapped with joy and made a crazy squeaking noise that must have been some kind of bird language. Vee laughed at Tabitha, but when her father offered her the delicious looking desert, she just put up her hand. She'd lost her appetite. Something wasn't right. What could it be? Images from the past summer flashed through her mind. Lily and Olivia had gotten into a lot of trouble sneaking out of their hotel room with a guest player named Colby. They'd both been grounded and nearly suspended from the team. Olivia never seemed really sorry for what had happened and even called Vee a baby for not joining them. The fall season had started tense, but ended smoothly. Vee prayed that the drama from the summer was gone for good. She needed her team to stick together.

"*M'ija*?" Tomas asked again, the lovely flan in front of her.

"No, *gracias, Papi*, I'm just not hungry."

Chapter 4.

Perhaps the only thing Vee loved as much as playing soccer with her team was watching soccer with her father on Saturday mornings. The two were relaxing on the love seat in the living room of their apartment while English Premiere League soccer blared from the small television. She'd invited Lily over to watch the match, but Lily said she couldn't because she had to do some chores around the house.

She's missing a great game, Vee thought, sighing contentedly as her father massaged her foot. She closed her eyes for just a second, but then felt an extra-hard squeeze right in the bottom of her foot.

"Ouch!" Vee cried, as she wrestled her foot away from her suddenly agitated father.

Tomas dropped her foot and stood up to yell, "*Es una falta*!!!"

"What happened?" Vee asked, rubbing her foot. She watched the slow-motion replay and, sure enough, saw her favorite player brought down by a wicked tackle, just outside the 18-yard penalty box.

"That was totally a foul!" Vee shouted, jumping to her feet. "How could they not call that?"

Both Merinos were outraged. Play on the pitch continued, even as Javier Hernandez lay on the ground, rubbing his ankle, his face grimacing in agony. Vee checked how much time was left in the game by looking at the box on the upper left-hand side of her screen. Just five minutes. The score read Manchester United 2, Chelsea 2. Tied. Manchester United needed to win this game to stay in first place. A tie was only worth one point in the standings, but a win was worth three.

"Please get up, Chicharito…" Vee muttered. Javier Hernandez was her favorite professional player in the whole world, and she knew he was the one guy who could get Manchester United back in the game.

Tomas laughed a bit and said, "*No te preocupes, el es muy fuerte.*"

"I know he's strong, *Papi*, but he's also still on the ground." Vee inched closer to the television, as if he could feel her presence. Hernandez was writhing in pain. Vee could see his nickname embroidered on the back of his shirt, "Chicharito." Like many professional players from Latin America, he went by just one name.

A Manchester United teammate finally kicked the ball out of bounds to give Chicharito a chance to get back on his feet. Vee was relieved to see him start to get up, but didn't like the fact that the clock kept ticking.

Vee sat back down next to her father, who rubbed her shoulders this time. Vee smiled at him. Saturday mornings had always been their special time. But for the last few years, it had become even more exciting because Hernandez was one of the first Mexican players to emerge as a European superstar.

Tomas had explained where Chicarito got his nickname: Hernandez's father and grandfather had both been soccer stars in Mexico and went by the name "Chicharo," which means green pea. Tomas said it was because of the grandfather's green eyes. Chicharito means "little green pea," and that's the name that stuck when the grandson became a world-famous player.

Tomas got up from the couch and went to the other room in their small apartment.

"*Papi*, the game's back on!"

Vee could hear him rummaging in a plastic bag. He walked back into the room and tossed a dense packet at Vee.

It bounced on the floor and settled at her feet. Vee picked it up and knew immediately. New practice socks.

"*Gracias, Papi.*" Vee said with a smile, turning back to the game and tearing open the plastic bag filled with two pairs of white soccer socks. Vee glanced at the clock and felt another jolt of excitement. Tabitha should be here any minute. At the last minute, their coach had found a field and the Bombers had avoided a forfeit. They were playing at another indoor turf facility in a neighboring town.

Vee pulled out a pristine pair of new socks and rubbed her fingers across the soft, cotton foot. Her father had remembered to get the extra soft kind. She glanced at Tomas as he watched the game, flooded with feelings of safety and love. But soon enough, action on the field re-grabbed her attention. Man U was on a flying counter-attack in the game's waning seconds. Robin Van Persie, the other star-attacker, had the ball in the corner. He pulled it back with his left and lifted a right-footed cross into the box. Chicharito was there, but Vee could tell he was at an impossible angle. Even if he could control the ball, he couldn't shoot. Chicharito had his back to the goal and the opposing team's defenders surrounded him, pecking at him like angry chickens. Chicharito brought the ball down and guarded it with his body. He looked for an opportunity to shoot. Vee stole a glance at the clock. They were in injury time already. Thirty seconds to score or Manchester United would suffer one of its first ties of the season, letting their nemesis and rival, Manchester City, take the lead for first place in the Premiere League.

"Do something!" Vee yelled at the television.

As if he could hear her in cold, rainy England, Chicharito made his move. He faked to his right then turned to his left. And instead of going for the impossible shot, he flicked the ball away from the goal with the outside of his left foot. The ball rolled slowly until a blur in red barreled his way into the box. The blur was Van Persie. He crunched a left-footed shot, the ball rocketed toward the goal and slammed into the back of the net.

"Goooool!" Tomas and Vee shouted together as Chicharito and Van Persie celebrated yet another amazing, jaw-dropping, come-from-behind victory.

All of sudden there was a pounding on the door. "Vee!"

Vee shot to the door and opened it quickly.

"What the heck is going on in here?" Tabitha asked with a laugh. "Did I miss our game or something?"

In their celebration, Tomas and Vee hadn't heard her knocking.

"Man U just scored in injury time!" Vee told her, grabbing her bag and ball. "Bye *Papi*!"

"*Tus tacos!*" Tomas yelled after her. *Tacos* was Mexican slang for soccer cleats.

Vee looked down to see she was only wearing her new white socks. No shoes.

"I'll put my shoes on in the car!" Vee answered running out behind Tabitha, scooping up her indoor shoes on the way out. Her socked feet felt the cold as soon as she hit the pavement. A small archipelago of snow and ice dotted the sidewalk. Vee hop-scotched around the ice patches, making grunting noises along the way.

Tabitha watched her silly friend wind her way to the car with a bemused look on her face.

"You look like a drunk frog," Tabitha announced, holding open the door to the big black sedan.

"Yes, I do, BUT, my socks are still dry!" Vee proclaimed.

"You know, you could have just put your shoes on in the house. We would have waited for you."

Vee smiled and shrugged. "Dude, way more fun this way."

Tabitha opened the back door to the car and the two girls got in.

"Nice hopping," was the first thing Vee heard. It was a male voice, but certainly not Rini's.

Vee looked to the front seat. Mark Gordon was

smirking at her. Vee was mortified. When Tabitha said "we" she thought she meant her and her driver, Rini. She had had no idea anyone was watching her lurch down the sidewalk, much less Tabitha's older brother Mark, aka Mr. Cool. She'd passed him in the halls at Tabitha's house a few times, but had never really talked to him. The way LJ had described him, you would have thought Mark was a Malfoy-wannabe in a Brookville letterman's jacket. Vee sized him up from the back seat. He certainly had Malfoy beat in the looks department, Vee had to admit. His hair was dark and on the longer side, sort of flopping across his forehead. He was looking down at his phone and playing a game or texting someone so she couldn't get a look at his eyes.

Vee gave Tabitha a "what-up-with-brother-in-the-front-seat look."

"Oh," Tabitha shrugged, getting the gist of Vee's quizzical look. "Turns out that Brookville Lacrosse has their games at the same place as our new field, so it's works out great. Rini can drive us both, no problem."

"Yeah, great," Vee answered quietly, putting it all together. She wasn't sure how she felt about going with Rini to practice several times a week. Something about being in Tabitha's super snazzy car made her feel uncomfortable. She also felt oddly relieved that her father wouldn't have to be part of the Bombers carpool.

"So did your little green bean save the day again?" Tabitha asked. Vee's love for Chicharito was no secret.

"Green pea! Not bean!" Vee whispered. She was appalled, but kept her voice down because Mark was in the car.

"I can't believe he scored another game winner!" Tabitha said.

Vee was about to respond when a voice from the front seat interrupted, "Actually, Van Persie scored the goal."

Mark held up his smart phone. Vee peered closer and could see Mark had been watching the game.

"Well, Chicharito assisted," Vee blurted out.

"True, but they should never have been losing in the first place. They are cutting it awfully close, if you ask me." Mark said.

Vee hadn't asked, but she was impressed. She didn't want to admit it, but she also agreed with him. Her favorite team was giving her high blood pressure lately. She couldn't even count the times the guys in red had had to score in the last seconds just to avoid a defeat or a tie.

"You watch soccer?" Vee asked, unable to help herself. Most of the Brookville boys she knew only like the big three: NBA, NFL, MLB.

"Our uncle lives in London," Mark said by way of explanation.

"You like Man U?" she asked tentatively.

"I'm a Man City fan, actually. But I keep an eye on the competition," Mark answered. Vee contemplated this information. Manchester City and Manchester United were archrivals. Both teams came from the same city in the middle part of England and were invariably battling for first place. Vee had heard that a Man City fan and Man U fan couldn't even travel in the same car over in England without coming to blows!

Vee settled into the back seat, unsure of what to say next. This called for some serious observing. She decided it would be a good idea to get her shoes on while digesting this new information about Tabitha's brother. She opened her bag and took out her indoor shoes. The bag tipped and her old, ripped socks and the camouflage bandana came spilling onto the seat. Vee quickly tried to shove them back in.

"These are nasty," Tabitha said in a non-judgmental tone, pointing at her old dirty socks. She picked up the bandana. "But...I still think this looks pretty cool."

Vee got her shoes tied and grabbed the bandana, this time tying it around her ankle. "How's this?"

"Even better," Tabitha answered.

Vee could see the parking lot for Total Sport. It was jammed with SUV's and helicopter parents. Vee could never handle the hovering types. Helicopter parents are the ones who study every minute of every practice. They don't even bring a book. They watch every second as if they could will a clumsy kid some skills. They are the moms or dads convinced they know more than the coaches, who scream at the referees, and generally embarrass their kids about fifteen times worse than your average parental unit.

Vee felt sorry for all those kids, some of them already teenagers, whose moms were still running up to them with tissues for a runny nose, or forgotten hair bands for a pony tail. All their fussing might as well might as well be like wearing a giant sign that read, "My kid can't take care of him or herself." Exactly the wrong message to send, in Vee's opinion.

Vee was so relieved Tomas wasn't like that. Sure, he worried when she forgot her pants in 12-degree weather, but to Vee, that was just being a good parent. He let her make mistakes and he also let her make her own decisions about most things. Rather than a helicopter, Vee considered Tomas more of a trapeze parent. He had enough faith in her to watch her fly high, but was always ready with the safety net in case she took a header down to the ground.

"Hand me Bubba," Mark said to the back seat in general.

44

Vee glanced around for something that might fit the bill. She saw Mark turn back and thought he looked impatient. In the silence, she tried to come up with something witty, "Uh … Bubba? Where are you? I don't see any lost dudes back here."

Vee could see a small grin flash across Mark's face. Tabitha laughed outright.

"Bubba is the name of his lacrosse stick," she said, picking it up from the floor of the back seat.

"Oh, right, of course," Vee said, with a chuckle. "Nice to meet you, Bubba. Sorry if I was stepping on your head!"

"Oh, Bubba's tough, don't worry," Mark said from the front seat, patting the netting of the stick. "Not too many brains in there anyway."

"Seriously, your lacrosse stick has a name?" Vee asked.

"Oh yeah, this is Bubba. Webber is at home. He is a little under the weather. And Thor is retired. He won the League cup a few years back with a game winner."

"Ah, yes, I see," said Vee, pretending to understand.

"Have a good game everyone," Rini said from the driver's seat. "Bubba, keep the fouls down."

Vee, Tabitha, and Mark piled out of the car and hustled into Total Sport, which resembled a chaotic airplane hanger. The sides of the building looked like a metal barn. They were red and massive, and the entrance was congested with throngs of parents and kids all trying to enter and exit at the same time. Bags, sticks, and balls clanged their way in and out of the building. Vee was surprised that Mark held the door for them both to enter first.

Through the crowds, Vee was relieved to see the Bombers gathered on the closer field.

"I have to make a pit stop," Tabitha said and headed to the bathroom. Vee jogged over to Olivia, Avery, and LJ, who were passing the ball around.

"Hey guys," Vee said, as she dropped her bag and bent down to check her laces and shin guards.

"Where'd you come from?" Olivia asked in a friendly tone that Vee was relieved to hear.

"I got a ride from Tabitha, but the parking lot was totally jammed. She's in the bathroom."

Vee carefully went through her pregame routine, including getting warm enough to do her important injury prevention stretches. Vee had sprained her knee badly during the summer and it had taken weeks for it to heal. The doctor said it was just dumb luck that she didn't tear her Anterior Cruciate Ligament. There was no more terrifying injury for a soccer player than an ACL tear. The physical therapist taught Vee how important it was for her to warm up before she played and to strengthen the muscles in her legs to prevent future injuries. No medical advice has ever been taken more to heart. Vee was meticulous about caring for her knee. Plus, she found doing the exercises before she played helped her relax.

"Don't take forever!" LJ teased.

Vee finished sticking her laces into the sides of her socks when she heard someone calling her name.

She looked around, assuming the male voice was her coach, but instead was surprised to see Mark Gordon walking her way.

Puzzled, Vee jogged over to meet him.

"What's up?" Vee asked.

"Isn't this yours?" Mark asked, holding out the bandana.

"Oh yeah, thanks. I guess it fell off somewhere."

"It was by the door. It's a zoo getting in here at changeover." He was right. When the exiting teams and the arriving teams all tried to jam through the door with their bags, it was chaos.

"Yeah, that was crazy." Vee bent down to retie the cloth around her ankle. She was surprised to find Mark still standing there. She looked up at him.

"Good luck in your game today," Mark said.

"Yeah, you too," Vee replied. "Have fun with Bubba."

"Oh, yeah. Bubba and I are gonna make some magic," Mark said with a smile and then turned back to his field.

Vee's eyes lingered on Mark as he sauntered back toward the lacrosse field. He wasn't at all what she had expected, she thought. And, she noticed, he had green eyes. She got up to rejoin her team when Olivia intercepted her.

"What was that all about?" Olivia demanded.

"What was what all about?" Vee was taken aback.

"What were you and Mark Gordon talking about?"

"Nothing."

"I saw you, Vee," Olivia said in an agitated tone.

"We weren't talking. I dropped something; he was just giving it back to me."

"What, some ripped old socks?" Olivia asked.

"What are you talking about? Why are you being so weird lately?" Vee finally blurted out.

Vee hadn't seen Tabitha jog over. "Who's being weird about what?"

Olivia didn't answer. Instead she just turned away and in a saccharine voice said, "Oh, nothing. Come on Tabitha, let's pass."

Tabitha shrugged her shoulders and grabbed her ball. Vee scrunched up her face and furrowed her brow. She was certain something was up now, and she was determined to find out what.

Chapter 5.

"Ready?" Lily asked.

"Actually, yes I am. Believe it or not. I already checked my laces, did all my stretches, and checked my headband. Twice."

"Very impressive!" LJ replied.

The two girls took to the field and started short one-touch passes, getting their bodies and minds ready to play. Vee tried to shake off Olivia's behavior. She had to focus on the game.

"I've never heard of this team, 'El Fuego'," Lily said after a stray pass went off to the side. "Have you?"

"Nope." Vee answered, backing up a few paces and sending Lily a high, loopy pass. Lily moved forward to take the ball out of the air, deftly bringing it down on her right foot. Vee checked out the opposition. They were in bright, neon orange uniforms with cool green and white striped socks.

"I like their uniforms," Vee commented.

"Yeah, pretty cool," Lily agreed, sending a long ball back Vee's way.

Looking closer, Vee thought she recognized one of the El Fuego players. She had middle length black hair, similar in color to Vee's.

"I think that girl might go to my school?" Vee said in a puzzled voice. "Or she used to."

"I think her name is Gabriela, or something like that," Vee tried to remember.

"Well, they look pretty good," Lily said, trapping a sharp pass from Vee.

Vee watched Gabriela and her teammates laugh as they played keep away on their side of the field. A blue and white ball passed in front of her. It was Olivia's ball. By now, it was obvious Olivia was bothered, but she had no idea by what. Vee passed the ball back and turned her attention from her opponents to her teammate. She watched Olivia make a strong pass back to Tabitha and then laugh when Tabitha made an awkward trap. Well, Vee thought, she looks pretty happy now. She just seems mad at me. I better talk to her. This is silly. We're Soccer Sisters after all. We're friends. Plus, we live by the code. Code #3 is very clear: Play with each other and don't take the fun out of it.

Soccer Sisters Team Code

1. Team first.
2. Don't be a poor sport or loser.
3. Play with each other and don't take the fun out of it.
4. Never put someone down if they make a mistake.
5. Practice makes perfect.
6. Never give up on the field or on one another.
7. Leave it on the field.
8. Always do the right thing.
9. Bring snacks on assigned days.
10. Beat the boys at recess soccer.

Go Bombers???

Vee hadn't thought of the code for a while. The team had written their ten sacred rules one day last year when practice was rained out by a freak thunderstorm. They all crammed together into Mrs. Dwyer's Suburban and came up with ten rules they all swore to live by.

"Uh, hello?" Vee heard Lily call from across the field. Vee hadn't even noticed she was frozen on the spot, observing Olivia and forgetting she had the ball at her feet.

"Oh, sorry," Vee said, sending a pass back to LJ. "I was just thinking."

"About?" LJ asked coming closer.

Vee knew that she should tell Lily about Olivia's odd behavior. It might not be an official Code, but Soccer Sisters don't keep secrets, Vee thought. The referee blew the whistle indicating it was time for the girls to take the field.

"I'll tell you after the game," Vee said. "It's no biggie."

"Okay, don't forget. I have to leave right afterwards for Billy's game," Lily said with a roll of her eyes. Billy was Lily's little brother, who as it turns out, was becoming quite a little soccer star himself.

"It's nothing," Vee lied.

Lily shrugged her shoulders. The girls took their spots on the field. Vee promised herself that she would find a way to talk to Olivia no matter what.

As soon as the referee blew the whistle, Vee could tell El Fuego was an excellent team. El Fuego started with the ball, passed it back, keeping control for what must have been a record for U13 girls soccer. The ball went from the striker, a slight girl with amazing ball skills, to the midfield, to the defense, and back up again. Player to player, pass by pass, El Fuego moved the ball without the Bombers even getting a foot on it.

Vee and Lily were stunned, and all the Bombers a little frustrated. It was sort of embarrassing not to be able to even touch the ball! Luckily, El Fuego seemed happy to play keep away and didn't do much attacking. After what felt like a long time, Avery was finally able to intercept a pass and get the Bombers in the game.

"Down the line!" Vee heard Tabitha yell and saw her long blonde hair flapping behind her as she darted downfield. Lily had the ball at midfield and was looking for a pass. She gave the ball to Vee, who immediately had two defenders on her. She tried to get the ball to Tabitha, but it went out of bounds.

"*Hola*," a girl said to Vee as the two teams waited for Tabitha to retrieve the ball.

"Uh, hi," Vee answered. It was the girl she recognized from school.

"I'm Gabriela," she offered. "We used to have Algebra together."

"Oh right," Vee said, feeling a little uncomfortable chatting in the middle of a game. A defender from

Gabriela's team took the throw-in, and again El Fuego passed the ball around like they were practicing some kind of cone drill. And the Bombers were the cones. This time, however, they wasted no time attacking. Gabriela and her teammates moved the ball so beautifully, they got a shot off and past Beth before most of the Bombers could even react.

"Let's go girls!" Chris coached from the sideline. "Wake up out there! Vee, less chatting, please!!"

Vee was mortified. Chris had seen her talking to the other team. What had she been thinking? Vee moved into position, ready to even the score. Lily started with the ball and this time, it was the Bomber's turn to wow the crowd. Lily and Vee moved forward in tandem, Vee darting forward after every pass, and Lily finding her feet every time. Tabitha flanked them out wide and Avery made a run to the far post.

"Drop!" Vee heard Olivia call, which meant she wanted Vee to pass the ball behind her. Vee turned and got the ball to Olivia.

Olivia crossed it to Tabitha who first-timed it into the box. Vee and Lily both pounced. Vee got there first, but again, defenders immediately surrounded her. Vee flicked the ball with the outside of her left foot to Lily who was in position to shoot. It was a perfect pass! Lily drilled it with her right foot and, just like that, The

Bombers and El Fuego were tied 1-1.

Vee and Lily hugged and the rest of the Bombers ran over to give LJ a hi-five.

"Hey, great cross," Vee said to Olivia, offering her hand, but Olivia brushed past her and ran over to give Lily a hug.

"Dude, seriously," Vee muttered to herself. Olivia's behavior was really bothering her now, but she had a game to play.

"Hey, great pass," Gabriela said to Vee, as they got ready to restart.

Vee wasn't used to her opponents handing out compliments.

"Oh, thanks," Vee said, thinking that El Fuego was a pretty nice team.

Gabriela smiled, but then both girls put on their game faces and got back to work. Vee really had to struggle to make anything happen during the rest of the game. It seemed like every time she got the ball, there were two defenders on top of her.

"Dude, they are all over me," Vee said to LJ.

"They are actually," Lily agreed. "They must have scouted our team before the game or something."

Sure enough, the next time Vee got the ball, she heard several of the El Fuego players yell something and realized they were talking about her in Spanish. A jolt of excitement and pride shot through her.

Again, two defenders surrounded Vee and sent the ball wide.

"What do you guys call me?" Vee finally asked Gabriela.

"*La abeja*, of course," Gabriela answered with a smile.

"The bee?" Vee laughed.

"Si, you are fast, buzz around, and have a nasty sting," Gabriela answered with a smile. "With the ball of course."

Vee had to admit that she was flattered. El Fuego thought enough about her as a player to give her a nickname and make sure there were defenders on her at all times. She didn't mention to Gabriela that Vee the Bee was exactly what LJ liked to call her also.

Vee decided it was time to live up to her name. She knew that if two girls were assigned to cover her, then someone on her team was always open. The key was to figure out who that was. Vee decided that she would get the ball and hold onto it, drawing as many defenders to her until she could find the open Bomber.

Vee had to give it to El Fuego; they knew how to pass the ball. While the Bombers were also great passers, she saw it was definitely something her team needed to work on. After a rare bad pass, Vee stripped the ball from Gabriela at about midfield and broke free toward their goal. She could feel the defenders closing in on her as they had all game. Vee held the ball close and protected it with her body, while trying to look up and find the open player. Now she had three defenders on her. She moved quickly left and right, not really trying to get to the goal, but just holding the ball long enough so that her team could get into scoring position.

"Now! Now! Now! Vee!" she heard LJ call as she made a diagonal run in front of Vee. Naturally, Lily James was her open player. Vee fed her the ball and

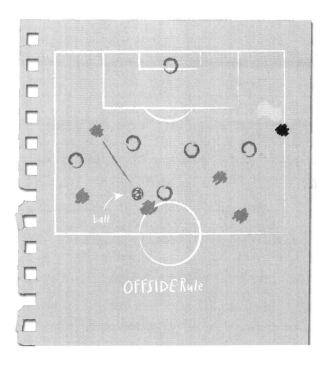

ball

OFFSIDE Rule

watched as she took off toward the goal. She raced after her, keeping an eye on the last defender while being careful to stay onside. In soccer, the attacking players have to stay even with the last defender until the ball is kicked, or else they are offside.

It's a tough rule to learn and even experienced players get called for a foul. For Vee, getting caught offside is the worst mistake. It means she hasn't been paying attention or observing what's going on around her. When the linesman sees a player offside, he or she raises their flag, the whistle blows, and your team loses both the ball and its chance to score. It's downright embarrassing.

Getting caught offside was something Vee tried to avoid at all costs.

"Send it long, LJ!" Vee called.

Lily sent a looping pass over the defense and Vee ran onto the ball, making sure she was not offside. No flag went up, no whistle blew. She gathered the ball at full sprint and crossed into the 18-yard penalty box. Vee was about to shoot when she felt a tug at her shirt. El Fuego was fast too, and they had caught up to her. The defender cut her off. Vee juked left, but another orange shirt had come to help. She lifted her head to try and find Lily or Tabitha. She was surrounded. Vee pulled the ball back and realized she had no option but to dribble. Gabriela was next to try and stop her. One by one, Vee outmaneuvered the El Fuego girls, bobbing and weaving, until she found herself with a shot. Wasting no time, Vee planted her left foot in the ground and did nearly a 180 to shoot the ball with her right. Her shot wasn't hard, but it didn't have to be. It was low and on target. The El Fuego goalie made a beautiful dive, arms outstretched, trying to tip the ball out of bounds. But she couldn't reach. Vee's shot hit the side netting and the whistle blew.

Bombers 2, El Fuego, 1.

Vee and her Soccer Sisters celebrated their goal while the El Fuego girls just shook their heads.

Vee thought she heard one of them mutter, "unstoppable."

"Who needs a little green bean!?" Tabitha teased. "Eat your heart out Man U. We have our own super star right here!"

"Green pea!" Vee corrected, laughing.

Out of the corner of her eye, Vee spied the Brookville Lacrosse team watching the game and banging their sticks on the ground in approval. The Bombers would play for the indoor championship!

Vee beamed. She hadn't intended on dribbling through six players to score the game winner, but she had been surrounded.

The final whistle blew and the Bombers cheered their hard-fought victory. The teams lined up to shake hands and the coach of the other team made a point of stopping Vee in the line.

"You are a fantastic player, *señorita*," he said, in a voice that sounded much like her father's.

"*Gracias*," Vee answered, instinctively.

Vee stopped when she reached Gabriela. "You should come and kick around with us after school sometime, Vee," Gabriela said. "We're even thinking of trying to get the school to start a team. We'd love to play with you anytime."

"Thanks," Vee said, surprised at all the attention.

Chris shook hands with the coach from El Fuego. It was clear they knew each other.

"Girls, this is Kite Robinson. We played together in college. To both teams, I just want to say this game was beautiful to watch. It's one of those days that someone ends up winning, but really all the girls on both teams should feel like winners. Days like today are the reason we love this sport."

Vee lingered a little longer to talk with Kite and Gabriela for a moment as the rest of the Bombers moved to the sidelines to gather their bags and coats.

"Vee, let's go!" Tabitha called. Vee saw Tabitha and her brother waiting by the exit.

Vee hustled over, happy to see that Olivia was also

nearby. In all the excitement she'd forgotten to try and find out what was bothering her.

"I'm coming!" Vee said, picking up her bag.

"Hey, that was a nice piece of foot work," Mark said as Vee approached.

"Thanks," Vee said. "They were all over me. I was trying to find someone to pass to, but couldn't."

"Yeah, they were marking you really tight from the beginning of the game," Mark said.

"I guess," Vee answered, surprised that he had been watching. "They were good."

"Where are they from?" Tabitha asked. "I've never seen them."

"I guess they are a new team, actually some of them are from my town, and some of them go to my school."

"Cool," Tabitha said. "They were nice. Ok, you ready?"

"Ready," Vee answered. The trio started walking to the door when Vee remembered her promise to track down Olivia.

"Actually, guys, can you give me one second?" Vee asked.

"Okay," Tabitha said, stopping by the entrance and having to dodge all the incoming players.

"Hey, Olivia!" Vee called, running after her. "Wait up."

Vee jogged over and Olivia turned around.

"That was quite a game, huh?" Vee said.

Olivia didn't answer right away, but just glared at Vee.

Finally she asked, "Looks like you knew some of them. Do you?"

"I guess I do. One of the girls used to be in my math class I think. She's nice."

"Oh, you like them?" Olivia asked with a sneer.

"Yeah, why not? They were cool," Vee said, trying hard to figure out how to turn the conversation around. She wanted to ask Olivia why she was so mean to her lately, but fumbled for the right words.

"Olivia?" Vee finally asked, determined to find out what was wrong. "Is something the matter? It feels like you are mad at me. Did I do something?"

Olivia was quiet for a second. Then she answered. "Actually, yes, Vee. There is something wrong and it's time you knew it. None of the girls are brave enough to tell you the truth, but I will."

Vee was puzzled. "Tell me what?"

"Look Vee, you just don't belong on this team anymore. You don't go to our school. You don't live in our town."

"What are you talking about Olivia? Are you crazy?" Vee was angry.

"Things have changed, Vee. You just don't see it. I mean, your dad doesn't even help with carpool. And even if he could, do you really think Tabitha would be seen dead in that clunker he drives? You are always late these days. Look, I'm sorry to have to be the one to tell you, but everyone else is too scared to hurt your feelings."

Olivia clearly wasn't, Vee thought. She felt like someone had punched her in the stomach. What was Olivia talking about? She looked around for Lily, forgetting she had already gone to Billy's game. There was no way Olivia was speaking for her team, no way she was speaking for LJ. She looked for Tabitha, who was waiting by the door. Vee noticed she did actually look a little annoyed.

Could what Olivia was saying really be true? The Bombers didn't want her anymore?

"No. You are making all this up," Vee said firmly.

Olivia fired back. "I'm not, actually. No one wants to hurt your feelings, Vee, but face it. You don't fit in anymore. Though you fit in fine with that team we played today."

Olivia gestured toward the remaining El Fuego players. "Why don't you just go play with them?"

Chapter 6.

Vee half walked, half stumbled back to the car. She felt like a passenger on an amusement park ride. The serious ones you have to be taller than 54 inches to ride. Maybe sign a puke waiver. She felt Six Flags-sick-to-her-stomach.

Tabitha laughed when she saw her, probably thinking she was doing the drunken frog walk again.

"Let's get out of here," Tabitha said as Vee collapsed in the roomy back seat.

Vee only nodded.

Olivia had rendered her speechless. She'd launched her verbal bomb attack, flashed a fake sympathetic look, and walked away. Just like that.

Vee was trying to regroup. She knew Olivia was full of it. Totally and utterly mean and crazy. And wrong. Why did girls have to be so nasty to one another sometimes? Vee tried to whip out her observation skills, to view what Olivia had said calmly, but then another wave of OMG hit her right in the stomach.

"Oh, turn it up, Rini!!" Tabitha cried when she heard the new Katy Perry song on the radio. "I love this one."

Mark rolled his eyes and grinned at Vee as Tabitha danced around in the back seat. Vee tried to return his warm and sincere smile, but all her game euphoria had been wiped away like pretty snowflakes on a windshield. Smeared with one swipe of Olivia's bitter words.

Vee wanted to talk to Tabitha, but the music was too loud. Tabitha, oblivious, bopped around, trying to get Vee to dance with her. Vee's glazed eyes wandered around the plush car, the driver, and realized she'd been blind. She imagined what Tabitha would say in her father's old junky car, a giant hole in the floor, recipes everywhere. She wouldn't say anything, of course. Olivia was right about that. Vee knew that Tabitha was too nice. She probably felt sorry for her. She didn't belong in this fancy car with a driver. It made her feel like a fake.

Suddenly, Vee needed to escape.

"Hey, want to come over?" Tabitha yelled over the radio. "We can make up some dances or something."

Vee squirmed inside. She hated to lie, but needed to try and get her head straight. What she really needed was to talk to Lily.

"Oh thanks," Vee answered. "But actually if you can just drop me at LJ's, my dad's going to pick me up there later."

Tabitha turned her head to the side, "I thought LJ had to go to her brother's game?"

"Oh yeah, she did," Vee realized. Then improvised, "My dad was doing something in their kitchen."

Tabitha gave Vee a quizzical look, but shrugged and said, "Ok. No problemo."

Vee made sure all her old socks and bandanas and worn shoes were well contained in her soccer bag, then scurried from the car as soon as it came to a stop. For the first time she was embarrassed that her father worked for the family of one of her teammates.

"Bye, Vee," Mark said. She waved a quick and hopefully confident goodbye and ran up the front walk to the James' door. She rang the doorbell and pulled her jacket closed, praying there was actually someone home.

The big black car idled in front of the house. Rini was, of course, waiting to watch Vee go inside. Vee rang the doorbell again. She peered through the little glass windows on either side of the front door. Oh please, someone be home, she pleaded. Vee was banking on the fact that the James' family almost never all went to Lily or Billy's games.

The tinted window of the black car smoothly rolled down.

"Are you sure someone is home?" Mark asked from the passenger seat.

"Uh, yeah," Vee stammered, banging harder on the door.

"Okay," Mark said, but Vee could tell by the look on his face that he was unconvinced.

Finally, Vee heard a noise on the other side of the door. She knocked one more time as the door finally swung open and Pop Pop, Lily's grandfather, unleashed a tirade in Italian.

Vee couldn't understand anything he was yelling and thought she caught him muttering something about Final Jeopardy. But it didn't matter because he wasn't looking for conversation anyway. He just turned around and walked back to his den, leaving Vee alone in the entry. Vee could hear the television blaring. No wonder no one could hear the doorbell or Vee's knocking. Vee waved to Mark, Rini and Tabitha and closed the door.

"Lily?" Vee called as she reached the bottom of the stairs. "Anyone home?"

In any other house, it might have felt weird to be left unaccompanied by a cranky grandfather. But Vee loved the James' home. She'd been hanging out there almost all of her life. And whereas Tabitha's enormous house was perfect and spotless and modern, Lily's house just felt family funky. There were piles of life-papers, permission slips, recipes, and food and nature magazines stacked on the kitchen counter. There were bowls of fruit on the table and usually something good cooking on the stove. The James' house was a home and just being there already helped Vee feel a little better.

"Hi Vee!" a voice called from the top of the stairs. It was Lily's mom, Toni James. "Your father already finished fixing the stove. He went back to *Katerina's*."

"Oh. I was actually looking for Lily. Is she home yet?" Vee asked, hopefully, dropping her soccer bag on the floor.

"Actually, she's not. She is at her brother's game, if you can believe that one?"

Vee smiled. She'd always had a soft spot for Billy.

"She'll be home in not too long," Toni James said, turning to go back upstairs. "Make yourself comfortable. Pop Pop is probably watching TV in the den. Just be careful you don't talk to him during Final Jeopardy."

Vee tried to laugh, but her heart wasn't in it. It felt heavy in her chest. Her shoulders sagged and her head kept tilting down.

"Vee?" She asked. "Is everything alright? Did you guys lose today?"

Vee wanted to tell her everything, but something about being twelve clamped her mouth shut. She stood up straighter, lifted her chin and put on her best fake smile.

"Oh, everything is great! We won today…" she said in a perky voice, but it trailed off at the end.

"Are you sure you are okay? How's the knee?" Mrs. James asked.

Vee rubbed her knee instinctively, then stopped, "It's fine." She knew better than to get Lily's mom going. She didn't need any starter fuel to worry.

Lily's mom tilted her head to the side and looked down at Vee. Uh oh. She knows me too well, Vee thought.

"Why don't you get yourself a snack and then come up and help me while you wait for Lily?" she asked Vee. "I'm doing a special on the medical uses of honey."

Vee perked up, "Sure, that sounds fun, actually."

Walking into the kitchen, Vee could tell things had been moved around. All the normal cooking paraphernalia was scattered on the countertops and her father's tool bag was still sitting on the floor. She decided to skip the snack and made her way upstairs.

Mrs. James was in her home office. It was packed with butterflies, crickets, beetles, wasps, spiders, ants, termites, scorpions, and pretty much any other kind of weird bug you could imagine. Lily's mom was one of the world's foremost experts on butterflies, also known as a lepidopterist. She had her own webshow called Madam Butterfly's Journey, but it often featured other insects.

Vee watched as Mrs. James organized her supplies for the show. She had several display cases with various sized bees. She also had a wide array of honeys on the table, hence the sticky bit. Vee noticed that there was a good-sized bandage wrapped around Mrs. James' right hand.

"Did you cut yourself?" she asked.

"Yes, actually, I did. So silly. I was working in the yard, without gloves, and I reached down and scratched the top of my hand pretty badly." She lifted up her hand to show Vee. "It's actually the reason I am doing this show on bees."

Vee was confused. "What do bees have to do with your hand?"

"Well, when I reached down, I scratched my hand against a sharp rock and got two really serious gashes on the top of my hand. While not deep enough for stiches, they were pretty bad. The weird thing was they were about exactly the same size."

Vee was still a little confused and made a face.

Mrs. James smiled and continued, "So, I decided to do a little experiment." Slowly, she began to unravel the white gauze.

"So you know that honey bees make honey, right?"

"Uh, I got that part!" Vee said.

"Well, bacteria cannot survive in honey. It's just too thick. Too sugary. It also fights infection. So for thousands of years people have covered their wounds with honey. The ancient Egyptians used honey as a wound treatment as early as 3000 BC, and it's even been found in Egyptian tombs."

This was news to Vee.

"Seriously? I put honey on my toast. Or if I have a sore throat, my dad gives me hot water with lemon and honey."

"Right, when you drink hot water with honey, the thick sugary honey can make it hurt less. Some honey is also thought to have anti-bacterial fighting properties."

Vee tried to get a better look at Mrs. James' hand. It looked like a regular old bandage.

"So you put honey on your cut?" Vee asked.

She nodded. "I did. On one of them I put honey and then covered it with a bandage. On the other cut I put an antibiotic lotion. The regular old kind you get at the pharmacy."

"And you want to see which one got better faster?" Vee asked.

"Bingo," Mrs. James said.

"Have you peeked?" Vee asked.

Mrs. James smiled. "Well of course, I have to change the bandage every day to keep it clean."

"So you just squirted honey into your cut?" Vee was appalled. That really did seem awfully messy.

Lily's mom laughed. "No, no. You definitely want to use sterilized honey especially made for wound care. The kind I use is from New Zealand from a pioneering scientist named Megan Mallgrave, and it's called Manunka honey."

"Does the queen bee make all the honey?" Vee asked.

"Actually the queen bee doesn't make honey at all. She lays eggs. Up to three thousand a day. The workers make the honey from flower nectar. It's their food."

"Seriously?"

"Yep." Mrs. James turned behind her and picked up a small glass case. "Here I have a specimen of a Queen Honey Bee and a worker bee." She handed the case to Vee.

The queen bee was much longer than the worker, Vee could see. "This is so cool," she whispered.

"How do you get to be the queen?" Vee asked. Inexplicably, Tabitha popped into her mind.

"Well, the queen is just a regular bee that is fed royal jelly. That is what makes her turn into a queen."

"Royal what?" Vee couldn't believe what she was hearing.

"Royal Jelly. When a hive needs a new queen the worker bees feed a special egg with a special substance that is super nutritious and the egg develops into a queen. That special substance comes from a gland on their head and it's called Royal Jelly."

"Okay, this is totally freaky stuff," Vee said. She wanted to call Mrs. James "dude," but thought maybe that wouldn't go over well.

"*This* is just nature, dear," Lily's mother replied.

Vee was fascinated. She realized there was so much for her to learn about the world and it made her excited. Honey for a Band Aid! Royal jelly! Egyptian tombs! She felt thirsty for more. Vee couldn't wait for Mrs. James to remove her bandage and see which one of her cuts was healing faster. Vee was betting on the bees.

A door slammed downstairs, followed immediately by what sounded like a herd of buffalo bounding up the stairs, then yelling, "Mom! We're home! Mom!!!!"

Mrs. James' and Vee's eyes met.

"LJ's home," they said together with a shared smile.

"Can you wait until Lily comes up to take off the rest of the bandage?" Vee asked excitedly.

"Sure," Mrs. James replied. Spontaneously, Vee jumped up and gave her a quick hug. She had totally forgotten about all the drama at soccer and felt suddenly so grateful to Lily's mother. She couldn't wait to share it with her friend.

"Lily!" Vee cried, heading down the hall. "You gotta come see this!"

Chapter 7.

"Hey! I didn't know you were coming over. What's up?" Lily asked coming up the stairs. She was still in her uniform from the game.

"Oh, you gotta see this stuff, dude! Your mom is doing the coolest ..." Vee tried to finish her sentence but a blur of red hair, orange uniform, and nine-year-old energy came barreling past Lily like a ginger bull running through the streets of Spain.

"Hey! Watch it!" Lily yelled as her brother Billy pushed her to the side.

"MOM! MOM! MOM!" Billy screamed. Vee pressed her back against the wall to get out of the way.

"MOM! I SCORED THE GAME WINNER TODAY!"

Lily rolled her eyes at Vee and said, "Beyond annoying."

Vee laughed. Lily's younger brother Billy was pretty entertaining most of the time, but she knew that he drove Lily crazy. She liked to call him her "little bother." Vee was an only child and had always been a little envious that Lily had a brother. There was always someone else to hang out with. She would have loved to have a sister or brother, even if he was a bother.

"How was his game?" Vee asked.

"Oh, it was regular nine-year old soccer. Bunching up and stealing the ball from each other. At least Billy knows better than that."

"Did he score the game winner, really?" Vee asked.

"Yeah. It wasn't a bad goal, but now he thinks his name is Billy Messi or something. Like he was the first person in the world to score a goal."

Vee definitely heard a tinge of jealousy in her friend's voice. Lily did not like sharing the soccer spotlight with her brother. Vee tried to imagine Billy as the next Lionel Messi, an Argentine left-footer who played for Barcelona and is considered perhaps the greatest soccer player of all time.

"The next Messi?" Vee joked. "Maybe Nike will name a line of soccer shoes after him sometime soon?"

"Exactly," Lily answered, heading down the hallway. "With a big orange stripe like his crazy hair!"

Lily stopped in front of her mom's office and waved. Vee could hear Billy telling his mother the play-by-play of his goal. Vee couldn't admit it to Lily, but she was happy for Billy. For so long, Lily was the only member of the James family to get all the praise for her soccer playing. Lily stomped away.

"She didn't even ask me about my game!" Lily was annoyed; Vee could tell.

"Oh, I told her we won," Vee said quickly, hoping to assuage her friend.

"What did you want to show me before?" Lily asked, opening the door to her bedroom.

"Oh, your mom is doing totally cool stuff with honey and bees," Vee told her. "It's so awesome."

"Oh, right. Putting the honey on her cut or something weird like that?" Lily asked, bored.

"Yeah, dude, it's so cool."

Lily gave Vee a look that made it clear she did not think it was cool at all.

"My mom and her bugs." She rolled her eyes again. "Let's go hang out in my room."

Vee followed Lily into her room. Posters of famous soccer players were plastered all over the wall. Abby Wambach. Alex Morgan. Ronaldo. Messi. Vee had most of the same ones in her bedroom too, although Vee's room was about one-quarter the size.

Vee flopped on the bed and watched as Lily took off her shoes, socks, and shin guards. She was dying to hear Lily say that Olivia was out of her mind. That she had no idea what she was talking about. But, Vee also realized that she hadn't told Lily about all of Olivia's weird behavior lately. It was like Vee was the only one who was noticing. She didn't know where to start.

"Hey LJ, remember before the game when I said there was something I wanted to talk about?"

"Oh, yeah, right," Lily answered. "What's up?"

Vee searched for the right words. Even in her mind, Olivia's claim that they didn't want her on the team anymore sounded dumb and impossible. She didn't even want to say it out loud. But she knew she could talk to Lily. Lily was her best friend in the world. Lily was her Soccer Sister. Lily was her family. They shared everything.

"Well, it's just that lately, Olivia … "

Just as she was about to spit the words out, Lily's door burst open like a Navy SEAL raid.

"Where are my headphones?" Billy demanded, filling the room in an instant. "You had them last."

"Will you get out of my room?!" Lily barked at her brother, as he rummaged through her desk, opening drawers and shoving piles of papers and toys onto the ground.

"Give me my headphones and I'll leave," Billy grunted. He moved from the desk to the dresser.

"Stop touching all my stuff!" Lily yelled. "I don't have your stupid headphones."

"Oh, what's this?" Billy held up what looked like a camisole of some kind. "Is this a bra?" He cracked up laughing.

"Yes, it's a sports bra, you moron," Lily answered.

Vee could tell her friend was starting to fume. Lily had had temper problems in the past, but had learned to control herself. The true test of her newfound patience was often her brother, who could push all her buttons. Vee could tell he was blowing the limits, like a race car zooming through a school safety zone.

Vee tried to help. "Billy, I think I saw your headphones in the front entry," she said, hoping he would leave before Lily went nuclear.

No luck.

"What the heck is this?" Billy was in Lily's closet now. "Is this some kind of Halloween costume?"

Billy emerged from the closet with a dress on a hanger. Attached to the hanger was a dainty pair of high heels.

"Put that down!" Lily screamed.

"Since when are you prom queen?" Billy asked with a sour face. Clearly, he didn't approve of Lily's dress. "You trying out for a Disney Princess job or something?" Billy did a fake parade wave, and Vee stifled a laugh.

"It's my dress for the Snow Fairy Dance. Get your dirty hands off of it," Lily went over to wrestle the hanger out of his hands. The dress was pale yellow and made of flowing layers. The shoes matched perfectly. Vee had never seen Lily with anything like it.

"Wow!" Vee said, almost unintentionally. It was one of the most beautiful dresses she had ever seen.

Lily grabbed the hanger. Shoved her brother roughly out the door as he began humming the theme from Sleeping Beauty. Lily slammed the door shut, turned around, and began to smooth out the dress.

"You like it?" Lily asked, a little shyly.

"Dude, it's awesome." Vee said honestly. "Are those matching shoes?"

Lily nodded and flashed a radiant smile. Vee could tell she was excited.

"Where did you get it?"

"The mall," Lily answered.

"You and your mom?" Vee asked.

"No, I went with Tabitha and Olivia before practice on Saturday," Lily answered, putting the dress back into her closet. "Olivia spotted it in this tiny store. She said it went with my freckles."

Vee had no idea Lily had had an outing with Olivia and Tabitha. She felt rotten. Not only was she not invited, she hadn't even known about it. Something else felt weird too, but she couldn't put her finger on what it was.

"You bought a dress before you asked someone to the dance?" Vee asked.

"Oh, no, you know my mom would never let me do that," Lily answered, gesturing towards her mother's office.

Vee was confused. Did this mean Lily had asked a boy to the Snow Fairy Dance?

"You asked someone?" Vee was scared to hear the answer.

"Yeah," Lily answered casually. "I asked that kid from homeroom, Justin. It wasn't that big a deal after all. Some girls are freaking out, but I decided to just get it over with. Right in the morning. I told you, right?"

Vee didn't answer right away. She was trying to calculate what she was hearing. Trying to figure out what it all meant. Lily James, her best friend in the world, tom-boy extraordinaire, had asked a boy to a dance, shopped for a dress, and Vee knew nothing about any of it.

"Yeah, yeah," Vee played it off. "I'm sure."

Vee watched as Lily carefully hung the dress back in her closet. Vee thought back to what Olivia had said at the game. Maybe she wasn't making it all up? Maybe that's what Lily, Tabitha, and Olivia had talked about at the mall when they were shopping?

Something on the ground caught Vee's eye. It was a long black cord with a pointed silver tip. Vee grabbed the cord and started to pull. Something bulky started to emerge from under the bed. Vee knew immediately what it was: Billy's headphones. He loved to listen to rap music and Lily and Vee always laughed when he tried to sing the words. He mangled all the lyrics at the top of his lungs, unaware that everyone could hear him.

"Look what I found," Vee said, holding them up.

"Chuck 'em in the garbage," Lily suggested.

"I'll bring them to him," Vee said. She was happy for the distraction. She had been so certain that Olivia was dead wrong, but now the queasiness of doubt had returned. She needed to clear her head and then talk to Lily.

Vee exited Lily's bedroom in search of Billy.

"Oh, there you are, Vee," Mrs. James' called out as Vee passed her office. "Did you still want to see my big reveal? Did you tell Lily?"

Vee stopped walking. She stood in the hallway, holding Billy's headphones, feeling lost in a familiar place.

"I told Lily, but …" Vee felt shy about finishing the sentence. Mrs. James finished it for her.

"She wasn't interested?"

Vee shrugged. She flashed Vee a knowing smile. "Don't worry, Vee. Lately, Lily's been a little distracted. She used to be mommy's little helper, but now she thinks my work is boring," Mrs. James said, chuckling to herself.

"She said that?" Vee asked.

"Oh, no, of course not. She's growing up. Both of you girls are. Interests change, and I understand. She still pretends like she's interested, but I know she's not." Lily's mom paused for a moment. "Honestly, Vee, I think she just doesn't want to hurt my feelings."

Vee's head began to spin. She dropped the headphones on the ground.

"Vee? You look pale, sweetheart. Are you okay?" Mrs. James asked.

"Uh," she stammered, "I just remembered something I was supposed to do."

"Vee, what's the matter?" Mrs. James asked, getting up from her chair.

"I gotta go!" Vee turned and ran down the stairs, flung open the front door and started to run.

Chapter 8.

Vee ran. She sprinted through the frigid streets of tony Brookville, the leafless trees a blur through her tear-filled eyes. Manicured lawns and fancy houses for big families flooded Vee's peripheral vision, further proof of her outsider status.

She sprinted for another few blocks and suddenly felt a twinge in her knee. She knew she should slow down, but couldn't. She needed to feel the burn in her muscles. In her chest. She longed for physical pain to drown out her internal heartache.

She. Doesn't. Want. To. Hurt. My. Feelings. The words pounded in Vee's head each time her feet hit the pavement. She turned away from town and up the hill. She felt another sharp pain in her knee. The orthopedist had told her to always warm up before she ran. But, in this moment, she didn't care. She felt her whole world slipping away from her, and if she couldn't be a Soccer Sister, what did her knee matter anyway?

She pushed herself up a steep hill. Her heart

thudding in her chest. Flashes of her team, of her friends, of Lily and Tabitha, her coach, filled her vision. Olivia's words ricocheted through her mind. She saw a car approaching and slowed, veering to the right side of the road. She didn't notice the slick and icy gravel. The black ice. She was still wearing her indoor soccer shoes, which provided no traction. As the car passed, Vee's feet went out from under her. She tumbled, falling hard to the ground in a heap. Her hands were scraped and bloodied, she felt something pull in her leg and twist in her knee.

The car passed. She lay by the side of the road unnoticed - heaving, hurting, and defeated. The girl who would never give up on the field was ready to give up on the game. Vee lay by the side of the road, her exhausted body not yet feeling the cold winter air. Her hands stung and her knee ached, but a memory began to fill her mind. Her very first soccer game. Before travel soccer. Before she was a Bomber. Or a Soccer Sister. The first team she ever played on was part of a recreational league, where little six-year-old girls played against other six-year-old girls from the same town.

Vee struggled to remember the name of the team. She could see their bright yellow uniforms and remembered how insanely excited and proud she and LJ were to be able to put them on for the very first time.

The day of that first game was a different kind of memory. Sharper and brighter than most. Less images than feelings. A real uniform. Vee was part of a team. Even better, she and Lily were on the same team. How could it get any better? She knew her father must have arranged that. Vee remembered struggling to pull up her tube socks and get her shin guards in place. Forget tying her shoes. She hadn't even learned how to do that yet. Tomas did that for her too. They played that first game in the spring. It was chilly, but sunny. Most of the game was just a bunch of little girls chasing the ball in a giant pack. These were the days before passing and teamwork; soccer was nothing more than the disorganized, joyful exuberance of six-year-old energy.

She could still remember the feeling of running down the tiny field with her only mission: get that ball. Their coach was a woman named Stacey. She was kind and smart and a really good soccer player. She coached them gently but firmly, guiding them in a no-nonsense kind of way. Vee liked that she never treated them like babies. She taught them seriously, so they learned to take it seriously. At least some of them did. There were always a few lost ones picking at the grass and doing cartwheels across the goal.

Vee still could remember how Coach Stacey tried to break soccer down into the most simple of ideas: be safe on defense, be in control in the midfield, and take chances on offense. Soccer was simple. Beautiful. Uncomplicated.

Vee sighed. When did everything change? She wondered.

"The Daffodils!" Vee suddenly said out loud, to no one. All the girls' teams were named after flowers: the Daffodils, the Tiger Lilies, the Clovers. Vee also remembered that she, Lily, and the Daffodils had lost that very first game by some ridiculous score. Six to five, or something like that. Coach Stacey told them they had learned a very important lesson that day about defense and maybe they should start playing some. Vee smiled at the memory.

"The Daffodils," she said again. She sat up and rubbed her knee. Out of the corner of her eye, she noticed there was someone standing nearby, watching her.

"I don't think daffodils are quite in bloom yet, Vee."

It was Mark Gordon.

He was standing on the hill with a bemused look on his face. He had Bubba in one hand and a large red bag slung over his shoulder. Vee had no idea how long he had been watching her.

"Uh …" Vee stammered, totally at a loss for what to say. "Yeah. Uh. Actually I was just thinking about something."

Mark tilted his head to the side and grinned. "Do you always lie by the side of the road, in a pile of leaves, in the middle of winter, to do your 'thinking'?" he asked.

Vee couldn't help but laugh. She was covered in twigs and mud. She brushed them off and started to get up, wincing as pain shot through her upper leg.

"Ouch," she said, involuntarily grasping at her knee.

Mark moved quickly to help her.

"Are you okay?" he asked laying his lacrosse bag and stick down by the side of the road.

Vee's first instinct was to say she was fine. To pretend there was nothing wrong. But her rawness had left her incapable. Plus, he did kind of find her muttering to herself by the side of the road. So instead, she just told him the truth.

"Well, I'm having a particularly awful day," Vee's said, her voice cracking slightly. "I tried to run to forget about it all, and then I slipped and fell and hurt my leg, if you must know the truth." Her voice cracked again. "So no, I guess I'm not okay. I'm kind of a mess right now."

Mark nodded in agreement, then moved closer to offer his arm. He too slipped on the ice.

"Whoa," he said, steadying himself.

"It's slippery," Vee offered with a weak chuckle. "Black ice. It got me."

"I see that," Mark said. "Hang on a second." He reached back and grabbed his long lacrosse stick.

"Bubba, at your service," he said with a wobbly bow. He passed Bubba to Vee, and she grabbed ahold, lacing her fingers into the basket where the ball goes. He held it steady until she got past the ice and onto the road. He held her up by the arm as they stood on the steep hill.

"Thanks," Vee said sincerely. "I might have stayed there all day."

"No problem. But we better get out of the middle of the road. People come flying down this hill all the time." Mark said. "Where are you headed?"

Vee really didn't know. She shrugged. "I guess I'll just walk, uh, limp, into town."

"That works," Mark replied. "I'm going to practice some shooting at the school. I didn't have a very good practice today. I'll walk with you."

Vee and Mark maneuvered down the hill carefully. Vee's knee was still sore, but she felt like it was stable enough to walk on.

"So is that the same knee you hurt in the tournament last summer?" Mark asked as they reached the bottom of the hill.

"Yeah, it is. I thought I had torn my ACL, but I was lucky. It was a bad sprain, not a tear," Vee said.

"I hear about a lot of girls blowing out their knees," Mark said sympathetically. "Boys, too."

"I know. It's awful." Then something dawned on her. "How did you know I hurt my knee last summer?"

"Oh, my sister told me. She's obsessed with your team. It's, like, the only thing she wants to talk about."

"Really?" she asked. Vee was elated to hear this.

"Yeah. I pretend not to listen, but I know what's going on," Mark said with a laugh. "And by the way, last I saw you, uh, like two hours ago, you had just scored the game-winner in an awesome game today. That's not too awful a day, if you ask me."

Vee knew he must want to know how she went from glory to gutter in a matter of hours. She felt badly she hadn't even asked about his practice. She sighed and tried to explain, "There's just been some stuff going on with my team, off the field, that's getting to me."

Mark nodded his understanding. "My whole basketball team fell apart this winter because a few parents got into an argument over something dumb. One minute, you're a team and another minute, a disaster. It's scary how fragile it can be sometimes."

They walked in silence toward town. Vee's progress was slow, but Mark never complained or rushed her. He also didn't seem to mind when Vee stayed quiet. She was grateful that he didn't push her to explain more. Not that she could. Her emotions were as jumbled as a scattered deck of cards. Somehow talking to him was calming her down.

They approached town. Vee went into observer mode. Observing herself this time. She realized that she felt perfectly at home with Mark. It was as if she knew he wasn't going to judge her. Like she could talk to him about anything. Like he somehow already understood.

"Have you ever had a friend that just changed on you? For no reason?" she blurted out.

"Actually, yes. You know, Griffin, aka G-4?" Mark asked.

"How could I not?" Vee said with a laugh. "He nearly took me out with his bike a few years ago." A memory flashed. Vee had been walking down Main Street when G-4 nearly ran her over on his dirt bike. Instead of apologizing, he told her she didn't belong in Brookville. Lily defended Vee and kicked a ball at G-4's head, hitting a street sign across the street and getting into a mess of trouble.

"Right. That thing with LJ. Well, he hardly talks to me anymore, either. We still play on the same teams, but we just don't hang out anymore. You can't really be best friends with everyone, I guess."

They walked for a few more minutes in comfortable silence.

"Well, I turn here," Mark said, gesturing to the school fields behind him. "Are you sure you are okay?"

Vee knew she didn't have to pretend. "Yeah, I'll be fine," she said with a smile. "A little rest, a little ice, I'll be good as new."

"I meant with the team stuff," Mark said.

"I'm trying to figure it out," Vee answered. "Thanks for the hand. Uh, I mean the stick."

"Bubba and I are happy to help anytime," Mark answered.

Vee turned to go.

"Uh, Vee?" Mark called to her. She turned slowly around.

"Yeah?"

"You're not at all what I expected," he said.

Vee lifted her eyes to his. "You're not what I expected, either. You're actually pretty nice. For a Man City fan."

Mark laughed at that one, "I'll see you around."

Vee waved and turned to go, but then Mark called her again.

"Vee?" he said, stepping closer. "Hold on a minute."

"Yeah?" She asked, noticing the greenness of his eyes. Kind of like the ocean just offshore. Mark came closer, his arm reaching slowly behind her. Vee froze.

Mark leaned in and his arm touched the back of her head. He bent over and whispered, "Hey, Man U girl. You have a giant pile of leaves and a huge stick in your hair."

Chapter 9.

Vee was walking toward town, still picking twigs out of her hair, when she heard the familiar rumble. It sounded like a cross between a lawn mower and a hair drier, only not quite as powerful. Her dad's clunker.

Tomas pulled up alongside her.

"*M'ija.*" He said with a sigh. *M'ija* was what he always called her. My daughter, it meant. It was a term of endearment, a sweet nickname, or as he said it now, an expression of exasperation.

"*Por favor, niña. Dónde estabas?*" Tomas asked. Vee turned to the car. Of course he wanted to know where she had been. She was supposed to be at the restaurant right after the game. Hours ago.

"Did Lily's mom call you?" Vee asked, feeling guilty.

"*Si. Y Lily. Y Tabitha,*" Tomas answered. He was only speaking to her in Spanish, which Vee knew meant he was very mad, very worried, or very tired.

Tomas suddenly noticed there was a scrape on Vee's hand. Her pants were covered in mud. She was shivering.

"*Que paso?? Cuéntame.*"

He wants to know what happened. Oh, everything, *Papi*, she thought.

Suddenly, Vee was hit by a black wave of emotion. It was all too much.

Dude. Dude. Dude. Too many feelings. Too many complications.

> Her leg hurt. She was cold. She was really, really tired.

Vee longed for a simpler time. To be just a little girl and fold up into her father's arms again.

She started to cry.

Tears welled up in her eyes. They streamed down her cheeks and she sobbed a giant, "*Papi!*"

Vee didn't often cry. They both knew that. Tomas' anger immediately turned to concern and he pulled the car to the side, got out, and ran to embrace her.

"*No llores, hija mía, no llores,*" Tomas said, stroking her hair, plucking out the last of the leaves. Vee allowed him to guide her to the car. The tears continued to flow. Tears for her bruised heart, for her splintered pride, and for her girlhood that was quickly becoming just a foggy memory.

Tomas held her. He didn't ask any questions. He stroked her head and kissed her tears. When finally she calmed down, he found an old t-shirt from the back seat and wiped her face. She shook her head and laughed a little. Her dad and his car full of random junk.

"We should talk a little, no?" her father asked, gently. Vee nodded, getting into the front seat. Tomas put the car into drive and made a sharp U-turn. Away from town, but not toward home.

"Where are we going?" she asked, confused.

Tomas rolled his eyes, as if she should already know. "*A los* World's Most Incredible Hot Dogs, *por supuesto*."

Now Vee really started to laugh. That fragile laugh after a good cry. Her father, the talented chef, food expert, Mexican by birth and blood, was obsessed with American hot dogs. He loved them. He loved the toppings. He loved to examine the casings. He had opinions on sauerkraut. He had conducted taste tests, then deemed World's Most Incredible Hot Dogs in the Ridgeway Mall the best ever. The warmed, buttery buns were the deciding factor. Vee adored the way he always said "incredible" with an exaggerated Spanish accent, (*En-cre-dee-bee-lay!*) and the fact they always went there to eat when there were important family matters to discuss.

The ride was short and silent. The mall was buzzing as Vee and Tomas walked toward the restroom so she could wash her hands. She told her father that her knee was feeling better. Still sore, but functioning well enough. They passed the electronics kiosk, a Gap, and then a small boutique that caught Vee's eye. There were several girls her age loitering out front. She didn't recognize them, but one was wearing a Brookville Track t-shirt, so she figured they must attend Lily's school.

Vee smiled at the girls, who were texting and oohing and ahhing over a pair of platform pumps. Vee's pace slowed as she passed the shop. Vee's usual wardrobe consisted of comfy leggings and soccer jerseys, but seeing the dress in Lily's closet made her peer for a moment longer. Is this where she had come shopping? Without her?

Vee meandered closer to the boutique, whose doors opened up to the mall with racks of dresses and tops right out front. She stopped to touch the fabric on a navy blue dress. It was covered in tiny pieces of shimmering silk cut outs shaped like butterflies. The fabric felt fancy and the butterflies floated on the dress as if in mid-air. The dress looked elegant and whimsical all at once, grown-up but not too old. Vee thought it was kind of in-between.

Like her.

"*Te gusta*?" Tomas asked. Vee had forgotten he was even there.

"Yes," Vee answered. "It's beautiful."

"*Vamos a comprarla!*" Tomas said, happy to do anything to cheer up his daughter.

Vee smiled, but shook her head. "No, *gracias*. Come on. Let's go eat."

They found a quiet table in the back and Vee unloaded her troubles on her father as he loaded toppings on his three hot dogs.

Yes, three.

1) Traditional with sauerkraut with yellow mustard. The all-time favorite.
2) With onions cooked in ketchup (the smell of this one made Vee want to hurl).
3) A la Mexicano: his own creation. A foot-long, with hot sauce, raw onions, cilantro, and a touch of lime.

Vee shook her head as mustard dribbled down her father's chin.

"Okay," Tomas said, "*Cuéntame todo.*"

He wanted to know everything. Vee told him about how annoyed she was that her teammates were so obsessed with the Snow Fairy Dance. She told him how Olivia had been being mean to her at practices and she had no idea why. She told him how she'd tried to talk to Lily, but feared Lily just didn't want to hurt her feelings. She told him how she'd run to escape, fallen, and how Mark Gordon had helped her up and walked her to town.

Tomas seemed relieved. At least nothing terrible had happened when she was running through town. He put down the onion hot dog and said, "*Pero*, what could anyone say that could upset you so much, *mi amor*?"

Vee hesitated just a little. She felt the tears coming back.

"Olivia said that they didn't want me on the team any more. That Lily and Tabitha didn't want to hurt my feelings, but that things had changed."

"But Vee, you know this is not true. Did you talk to LJ? She is … *como tu hermana*." Tomas asked.

"I tried, *Papi*."

"Did she say this, too?" Tomas asked with a shocked looked on his face.

"No, she didn't say it, but … "

"But, *nada. m'ija*, you must have more faith in your friend. *Y Tabitha también*."

Vee hung her head a little bit. He was right. Why was she doubting her friends?

"*Papi…* " Vee continued. "We played against a team called El Fuego. They were Mexicanas, like me. They were so nice. They were really good, too. Some of them go to my school. A really cool girl named Gabriela."

"Ah, *te llamó una Gabriela hoy*," Tomas said, holding a finger in the air, making the connection.

"Gabriela called me today?" Vee asked.

"*Si*. She invited you to play with her after school. In the gym."

Vee nodded. "I think they might start a school team."

"*Bueno*," Tomas nodded, liking the sounds of Gabriela.

"*Papi*, Olivia told me that I should go play with El Fuego."

"*Cómo*?" Tomas wanted to make sure he understood.

"She told me that I didn't belong on the Bombers anymore."

"*Y porque*?"

Vee shrugged.

Tomas pushed his final hot dog aside. He spoke slowly and carefully in English. "You must ask yourself why this girl has upset you so much, no?"

100

Vee knew he was right. Tomas continued in Spanish.

"I have always worried that this day might come. That you might want to play on a different team from Lily. That you might want to play in your own town. The Bombers are a wonderful team. Wonderful people. Maybe not this Olivia, though. It has always been your decision to play soccer. You are so talented. Maybe it's not a bad idea to give it a try?"

Vee shook her head. "But *Papi*, I am a Soccer Sister."

Tomas raised his eyebrows. "Maybe Gabriela is also a Soccer Sister. *Una hermana nueva*?"

Chapter 10.

Vee and geometry were not friends. At least, not at the moment. Tonight's torture was equilateral, isosceles, and scalene triangles. Generally, Vee loved math, but on this evening she was having a hard time getting her thoughts together. Sitting alone at the big wooden table in the back of *Katerina's* surrounded by books, she mindlessly tapped her pencil on the table. Tap. Tap. Tap.

Okay, let me try this one more time, Vee thought. She refocused her eyes on the page and read aloud, "An equilateral triangle has three equal sides. An isosceles triangle has two equal sides, and a scalene triangle are all offside."

She copied it down and read it again. She took a closer look and groaned.

"Offside!?" she shouted. "Equal sides, not offside! Ugh!!!" Vee threw her pencil across the room and then laughed a bit when it stuck in the recipe corkboard.

The truth was, Vee could not get her mind off her

team. She slammed her book shut in frustration. Her father had suggested she skip practice tonight to give her knee a rest. Vee didn't resist. For the first time ever, she needed a break from her team so her head would clear. She'd called her coach to let him know she wasn't going to be there.

But now she was feeling adrift. She hadn't played soccer all week, hadn't talked to Lily. She missed her team, and she had to admit, she missed seeing Mark on the way to practice. Taking a break was for the birds. The truth was, her knee felt just fine. The ice and rest had done the trick.

Vee was dying to play. Gabriela had called again, and Tomas convinced Vee to agree to go kick around in the gym after school tomorrow. Vee could tell her father was really worried about her. He wasn't normally this involved. Initially, Vee was resistant to playing with the El Fuego girls. She felt a little guilty even considering it. But Tomas pointed out that it was just kicking around after school, and he reminded her that they were talking about starting a team at her school and would need her. Plus, Vee had to admit she liked Gabriela, and more than that, she really liked being wanted. Better than how she was feeling about the Bombers. Confused was putting it mildly.

She wondered if Lily had practiced her penalty kicks? She hoped that Tabitha was working on her defense. Those long ballerina legs had a tendency to stab at the ball. She tried not to think about Olivia, and how happy she must be that Vee wasn't there.

Vee pushed her math book aside and picked up her English novel, The Good Earth by Pearl S. Buck. It was a reading assignment about a family in China before World War II, and Vee loved losing herself in this family epic. She was almost done and hoped that Wang Lun and O-Lan would distract her.

"*¿Cómo estás?*" Tomas asked, sticking his head through the kitchen door. He had been checking on her every five minutes.

"I'm fine, *Papi*," she answered.

For the next few minutes she lost herself in ancient Chinese traditions, rubbing her toes occasionally as she read about how girls in China had their feet bound. Tied up in bandages to keep them small and dainty. It sounded like torture. Ouch. No girl soccer playing in those days.

The kitchen door opened again.

"I'm still fine, *Papi*!" Vee said, without looking.

"It's me," a voice said. Lily James came into the kitchen, plopping her backpack on the table. The entire surface shook.

"Man, this thing weighs a ton," Lily said with a sigh. "How's the knee?"

"Better," Vee said. "It's pretty much all better."

"Oh good, we are so totally going to need you this weekend. Chris found out who we are playing in the Indoor Championship and you will not believe it!"

"Who?" Vee asked.

"It's a team called The Showoffs."

"Oh, come on. Seriously?"

"Yep. Can you believe that?"

Vee shook her head.

"And it's really just a winter select team made up from girls from …" Lily did a drum roll with her fingers on the table. Vee held her breath. "… Castle Creek."

"Noooooo!" Vee said. Castle Creek was the Bombers' arch-nemesis. During the outdoor season, and at many tournaments, the two teams were constantly battling for first place.

Lily nodded knowingly and said with a smile, "We need you, dude."

Vee was so happy to see her friend. She couldn't wait to take on Castle Creek. She and Lily would make some magic up front and on defense Avery and Olivia would be solid…the thought trailed off in Vee's mind.

Olivia.

"And then we have the dance later that night," Lily said. "I hope I don't scrape up my knee on the turf. I already have a good one from last week and my mom keeps chasing me around with honey. It's, like, her new favorite thing."

Vee's laugh was a little forced.

She thought of the dance. Lily, Tabitha, and Olivia shopping. Vee had forgotten it was all happening this weekend. Oblivious, Lily lifted up her leg to show Vee the impressive turf burn on her right knee.

"Nice one," Vee commented. Then she noticed that Lily was wearing a bandana around her ankle. She pointed to it and asked, "Torn sock?"

Lily smiled. "No, you couldn't be there today so I wore a bandana. Tabitha did, too. It looks cool. We are thinking of wearing them to the dance!"

Vee sighed. Instead of being flattered by the bandana, she was annoyed by the dance, "Is everyone still talking about this? Jeez. It feels like this dance is way more important than our team, lately."

Lily nodded. "Yeah, I can't wait for it to be over. I'm so glad that I asked someone early. You should see how stressed out and obsessed everyone at school is. There are only a few more days. Olivia is the worst."

Vee had to admit she was happy to hear that one. "She didn't find her secret date yet? She wouldn't even tell me who she wanted to ask," Vee said. "Like I care,"

"Oh, get this one. Poor Tabitha is stuck right in the middle. Olivia finally fessed up that she is like, dying to ask Mark. She was supposed to do it after practice today. When I left, she looked so nervous, I thought she was going to throw up. She thinks he knows and is avoiding her."

"Mark Gordon?" Vee asked.

"Yeah, Mark. Mr. Cool. Tabitha's brother."

"Olivia is going to the dance with Mark Gordon?" Vee asked. Her voice was louder and more urgent. Suddenly she did care. A lot.

Lily answered, "I dunno. She said she was going ask him today after practice."

A wave of jealousy flooded her body. Vee tried to hide her shock. Olivia and Mark Gordon.

"LJ, there's something you should know," Vee said. She took a deep breath, "Olivia is the real reason I didn't come to practice today."

Lily looked confused. "I thought you were hurt?"

"No, I am…" Vee said. "I …was. But now I'm not. I'm fine."

"Wait. What?" This wasn't going well. Vee could tell Lily was getting upset.

Lily asked, "I don't get it. Didn't you tell Chris you hurt your knee?"

"No, no, no, I can play," Vee tried to explain. She didn't want to make Lily worried about the Championship. "See, look, I'm fine. I'm going to play tomorrow after school with El Fuego. I just needed a break today."

"El Fuego? What? What are you talking about, Vee?" Lily asked, her voice getting louder. "We have the biggest game of the indoor season coming up and you skipped practice today? All because of Olivia?"

Vee shook her head. "I've been trying to talk to you about this, LJ. It's bad. Olivia has been super-harsh to me lately."

"About what?" Lily was nonplussed. "She's been weird to everyone lately. She's sucking up to Tabitha to get to Mark, which of course, totally backfired. She's just totally out of control about this dumb dance. We're all sick of it."

Vee could tell Lily wasn't getting it. "But, LJ, it's not about the dance. After the last game, she said that I didn't belong on the Bombers anymore. She said because I live in a different town and go to a different school I shouldn't be on the team."

Lily scrunched up her face. Vee continued, "She said that you and Tabitha believe that too, but just don't want to hurt my feelings."

Lily narrowed her eyebrows. She stared at Vee. Her mouth hung open.

Vee waited for her to say something. The two girls stared at one another for what felt like forever.

Finally, Lily spoke, "Well, that is the dumbest thing I have ever heard in my life."

Vee was surprised to hear anger in her voice. Lily had more to say. "How could you believe THAT? Vee, you are my best friend in the whole world. You always have been."

"I know," Vee said.

"Do you really need me to tell you that? How could you believe I don't want you on our team? This is crazy." Lily's temper was as lost as a sunken treasure. She was talking with her hands and pacing around the small office. Vee was desperate for her to understand. "Well, you went to the mall with Olivia and Tabitha!"

"So what!" Lily yelled. "What does that have to do with anything?"

"You didn't tell me," Vee said. Suddenly, something about Lily's demeanor changed. She looked at the ground. She fiddled with her fingers.

"Why didn't you tell me?" Vee asked again.

"Well, I …" Lily stammered. "We just went right before practice on Saturday. It's not a big deal. I still don't see what this has to do with the Bombers."

"Hold on a second. You went on Saturday? Saturday morning?"

Lily bit her lip.

Tears welled up in Vee's eyes. She knew there had been more to this. She got it now. Saturday morning had been the Man U/Chelsea match. Lily had said she couldn't come watch because she had to do her chores. She had lied to Vee.

Vee looked at her friend. Lily looked back down at the floor.

"Vee … " she said finally. "I'm sorry … I just ……"

"Just what?" Vee asked in a small voice.

"I don't know. I guess I didn't want to make it worse that you weren't going to the dance. It sucks that we can't go to the same school. Plus, I know money is tight sometimes, too."

"So you lied to me?" Vee asked, crushed. She couldn't even manage a 'dude.'

"Look, I'm sorry," Lily apologized. "I didn't want to hurt your feelings."

There it was. Those terrible words again. Vee snapped.

"Let me get this right. You lied to me about shopping, because you didn't want to 'hurt my feelings'? So now, I'm supposed to believe that part, but not that you don't want me on the team. Maybe you don't want to hurt my feelings about that either? Don't you get it, Lily? That's exactly what Olivia said. Why can't you understand!!?"

"Because it's not true!" Lily shouted.

"Well, guess what? You can't just pick and choose

what I believe!" Vee said, her own anger boiling over. She got up to leave. She felt like her world was crumbling.

"You lied to me! I cannot believe you of all people would do that!" Vee gathered up her books and shoved them into her bag.

Lily tried to stop her, "Vee … Don't go!"

Vee paused for a moment at the door and looked sadly back at her friend, "You know, maybe Olivia is right. Maybe I don't belong anymore."

Chapter 11.

Game time was at 11am on Saturday. Vee turned on the television hoping to be distracted by Chicharito and Manchester United. She watched the last few minutes of the game. Manchester United was up by three goals, so Chicharito was on the bench. Sleet was falling. He looked cold. She wondered if he ever felt like the odd man out living in dreary, wet England. They probably didn't even have any good hot dogs.

"*Vámonos, m'ija,*" Tomas called from the hallway. They were headed to breakfast. It was almost 10am.

Vee was in limbo. She'd talked it over with her coach and her father and explained to Chris she wasn't sure she was going to play in the game today. Tomas filled him in on what had been going on with Olivia. Chris said he was going to have a talk with Olivia and hoped Vee would change her mind and come to the game. Vee knew her father also wanted her to play.

Vee walked slowly to the car. Her knee felt fine, but her insides felt tortured and twisted. She'd never been so confused. She waited for her father to unlock the door. The outside of the car was caked with winter mud. Taking her index finger she wrote, "Bombers," on the door.

"*Papi*, why don't you get a new car?" Vee asked. "We can't afford it?"

Tomas smirked as he got behind the wheel.

"I love this car," he said. "I will never give up this car."

Vee sighed, "It's a piece of junk."

Tomas started the engine, his smile spreading. He backed up, looking in the rear view mirror to make sure traffic was clear.

Finally, he said to Vee, "To you it is junk, to me, it is *un tesoro*. A treasure!"

Vee shook her head in disgust. She was pensive and quiet during the drive to breakfast. Images from her kick-around with El Fuego flashed in her mind. She had no idea what to expect when she showed up to the school field the previous afternoon. There were about eight girls there, some from school, but most from El Fuego.

"*Ya llegamos*," Tomas said, as he pulled into the small diner, their usual breakfast spot. Vee didn't hear him.

"*M'ija*?" Tomas asked again. Vee was lost remembering the warm welcome she had received from Gabriela.

"I'm so happy you are here!" Gabriela had said, even giving Vee a little hug. Vee couldn't help but notice it was a much nicer reception than she'd gotten from the Bombers lately.

"Oh, sorry, *Papi*," she said, getting out of the car morosely.

"Let me tell you about my piece of junk," Tomas said as they entered the diner. His accent made it sound more like "peeeas o yunk," than "piece of junk" and it caused Vee to snicker. Tomas scowled and lowered his voice.

He continuet in Spanish, "When I came to this country, I had nothing. Only you, my precocious daughter. I didn't have many skills. I didn't speak much English."

"Uh, you really still don't," Vee interrupted.

"Quiet child," Tomas scolded with a smile. "I had to find a way to take care of you and to survive. I worked in the restaurants because they would hire me. But I had a plan. I watched. I studied how to be a great chef. It wasn't easy, but I was determined to succeed. I had no choice."

The host showed them to their favorite booth. The waiter arrived with coffee for Tomas, juice for Vee, and a smile for his favorite customers. His name was Johnny and he knew there were no menus required.

"The regular?" he asked. Tomas and Vee nodded. Tomas always got the vegetarian omelets with a side of ham, and Vee, the blueberry pancakes with a dollop of whipped cream.

Tomas took a sip of his coffee and then continued his story.

"*Y lo logré*! I did it," Tomas said with pride, puffing up his chest. He continued in Spanish, "When I became the manager at *Katerina's,* many years ago, I finally had enough money to buy a car. No longer did I have to take the bus, or walk in the cold winter." Tomas took another sip and kept talking. "I went with the money my hard work had earned me and I bought this car. It was used. It wasn't perfect. But it was mine. I had earned it. I love it for what it stands for, *m'ija*, not for what it looks like."

The food arrived quickly, and Vee started to take a bite. Then, she put down her fork and said, "I'm sorry, *Papi*, for making fun of your car. I never knew that."

"Do not be sorry," Tomas replied, wiping his chin. "It is a terrible car. But sometimes, you just have to change the way you see something. When you see my car, you are embarrassed. When I drive my car, I am proud. You understand?"

Vee nodded. She did understand now. Vee thought again about Gabriela. She couldn't help but notice that they had the same exact hair color. The same color eyes. The same warm brown skin. They started with just a warm up game of keep away and Vee could see why they were such great passers. She met another girl named Ariella and a great dribbler named Nicole. Vee felt a little uncomfortable at first, but once they started playing, she just let the ball lead her and soon fit right in. They were a team full of joy, and friendship, just like the Bombers. She felt at home, like she belonged.

Tomas got up to pay the check. Vee fiddled with the straw in her orange juice. She knew her father was happy she had gone to play with El Fuego. She wasn't sure if he wanted her to play in the Bombers game today. To miss a Championship would make quite a statement, even if it was during the optional indoor season. Vee didn't doubt her love for the Bombers, or her bond with Lily and the rest of the team. Except, Olivia. Yet she had come to realize none of this would have gotten to her if she hadn't already had some serious doubts of her own.

Her father returned and together they walked outside. Vee knew the moment was coming. The teams were probably starting to warm up right now. She walked over to the clunker. The car she had been so embarrassed by. It was still old. It was still dirty. It really was still a piece of junk. But she could see now why he loved it. She loved it too now. She walked around to the back.

"We can never sell it," Vee said with a smile. Then she made a face and added, "But we can wash it."

Tomas nodded with a grin. "There is one more special thing about my car I want to show you," he said.

Vee was interested in hearing this one. Tomas pointed to the trunk. "It's in there."

"Open it!" Vee said, trying not to look at her watch, knowing it must be close to game time.

Tomas pressed the button to open the trunk. At first, Vee didn't see anything special. Then, she did. Her Bombers soccer bag. The Blue and yellow one with the awesome "Soccer Sisters" tag. She looked at her father.

"Now, *you* open it," he said. Vee obeyed. She felt the familiar joy of looking inside. There was her Bombers uniform. Her indoor shoes. Her shin guards. Her ball. A brand new bottle of water, and, of course, clean, beautiful new socks.

Vee sighed and asked her dad, "You think I should play today?"

"That is totally up to you. But I have never seen a longer or sadder face on my child. I think you should listen to Lily, not to that other girl, and I think you should listen to your heart."

He was right. Vee knew it the minute she saw her bag. While she was excited to get to know the El Fuego girls better and hoped they started a school team, in her heart Vee was a Bomber.

She smiled at her father. "*Gracias, Papi*," she said. She had had no idea he packed her bag.

They got in the car. Tomas turned to his daughter. He was beaming and had funny look on his face, a sort of know-it-all half-grin.

"Why are you looking at me like that?" Vee asked.

Tomas shook his head and raised his shoulders. "Oh, no reason. I just love you, *m'ija*."

Chapter 12.

Vee slipped into Total Sport unnoticed. She headed toward the locker room to get changed. She could see the Show Offs and the Bombers warming up on the far field. The sidelines were packed with spectators. She saw Tomas heading over to the field and wondered if LJ or any of the Bombers had spied him.

She slipped on her jersey, relishing the coolness of her number as it slid down her back, her protective soccer shield back in place. She sat on the bench and laced up her shoes, going through her special pre-game ritual. She could hear Lily's voice in her head, urging her to hurry up already.

Vee took a deep breath. She was ready. Ready to face Olivia and ready to face the truth. And the truth was that Olivia was a bully, and a good one. Her lies hurt so much because they had hit too close to home. Vee did often feel left out, she did feel vulnerable, and different, and she knew now this was an insecurity she would have to accept and overcome.

Vee checked her headband in the mirror, put her street clothes in her bag, and took a deep breath.

"Game on," she said to herself.

She slung her bag on her back, grabbed her ball and headed toward the field. LJ was the first to see her. She grabbed Tabitha by the shirt and pointed. Tabitha smiled and poked Avery. One by one the Bombers looked her way. Chris beamed as she approached.

As she got closer, she saw Lily hold up her fingers and heard her count…1,2,3. Then all the girls on the field screamed in unison, "DUDE!"

Lily ran over to hug Vee. Vee held her friend tight and at exactly the same time, they both whispered, "I'm sorry."

Lily pulled her back and said, "No sorries. You're here. That's what matters. I'm lost without you, Vee. I should have told you about my dress, and everything …I should have known you would have just been excited for me."

Vee nodded and then spied Olivia on the bench. She was openly glaring at them both.

Lily turned to look. "I'm pretty sure she's benched. When she got here today, Chris gave her a really long and special 'Think Time'."

"Oh brother, now she's going to hate me more," Vee said.

"Never mind her," Lily said. "She's got her own problems. Don't let her get to you anymore."

"I won't," Vee said firmly. Tabitha ran over to join them.

"Check this out," she said, lifting her leg all the way up to her head.

"You are freakishly flexible, Tabitha," Lily said with a shake of her head. "Like it hurts me to see you do that."

"Ballerina!" Tabitha replied with a giggle, and then pointed to her ankle. "We've all got them on. Here's yours."

Tabitha handed Vee a blue and yellow bandana that matched their uniform colors. "We got one for everyone and made Olivia wear one too. Ha!"

Vee looked at all her teammates and beamed. Each one had a bandana on her ankle. Any lingering doubts evaporated.

"Is the ref going to let us wear them?" Vee asked. Just then the whistle blew.

"We'll find out," Tabitha said with a smile. "Let's go!"

The Bombers took the field. Vee and Tabitha were up front. Lily took her spot in the midfield. Avery and Reese were on defense, and Beth was in the goal. Olivia was looking glum on the bench.

Vee sized up the Show Offs. Sure enough, Molly Barrelton, the Castle Creek superstar, was starting with the ball.

"Oh this is going to be fun," Vee said to herself. She made eye contact with Lily. Lily nodded. Vee the Bee was ready to fly.

The referee blew the whistle, and from the first moment of the game the Bombers were on fire. They were attacking from all angles, making incredible passes, and had so many chances to score. But by halftime, the game was still 0-0. They couldn't get the ball in the net. During the brief halftime, the girls only had a few minutes to grab a sip of water and switch sides. Vee grabbed her water bottle and took a long satisfying gulp.

"Why'd you even come back?" a voice asked. She knew it was Olivia.

Vee finished her sip. Took a deep breath and said, "I never left. This is my team, Olivia. I'm a Bomber."

"No one wants you here," Olivia tried again, a sneer on her face.

Vee replied with confidence. "Give it up, Olivia. I know you lied to me, so just save it. Lily knows. Tabitha knows. Everyone knows."

Vee felt a presence come up behind her. Lily James. Vee looked over her shoulder and went on, "I'm pretty sure the only one they aren't going to want around here is you. If you can't be a Soccer Sister, then you should leave. You don't have to like me. But I belong here and nothing you say will ever change that."

Lily put her arm around Vee.

"It's Team First, Olivia," Lily said firmly. "If you don't get that, then Vee's right. You're the one who doesn't belong."

Vee and Lily walked together back onto the field. Lily looked back behind her. "We'll see about her," Lily said. "We wanted Chris to kick her off the team, but he said she deserves another chance."

"I doubt she's going to change. I just hope I can play with her again. I honestly don't know," Vee said.

"Just remember Code #7."

Vee thought for a minute. She knew The Soccer Sisters Team Code by heart. "Leave it on the field?"

"Yeah, just play. Forget everything else. Just play… and leave it on the field."

She'd always thought that meant give it your all. Vee nodded. "Okay, I'll try."

The second half whistle blew and the Bombers were back in action. It took a few minutes for Vee to shake off what had happened at halftime. She knew that she was right about one thing. Vee was different. But different was great. She was proud of herself, her family, and where she came from and would never doubt her place on the Bombers or anywhere else again.

"Vee! I'm open!" Tabitha called from the outside. She was making a smart run up the flank. Vee fed the ball through two defenders and Tabitha went for the corner. She crossed the ball with her left foot, and Lily nearly got a head on it. They were getting closer.

The Show Offs got a goal kick because the Bombers' ball went out of bounds over the goal line. Molly Barrelton took the kick and it went all the way over the midfield line. That girl has a big foot, Vee thought. Their forward gathered the ball and Reese tried to chase her down. She went into for a tackle and missed. The ball went out of bounds, but Reese stayed down.

The referee called their coach onto the field, and Chris rushed to Reese's side. All the Bombers took a knee and then clapped when Reese was able to stand.

"I think she sprained her ankle," Tabitha said, walking over to Vee. They watched as Chris accompanied her to the sidelines. Their coach said something to Olivia, who jumped up from the bench.

"Oh great," Vee muttered. Olivia was coming in. Leave it on the field, she said to herself. Leave it on the field. Just play the game.

"*Vamos* Bombers!" Tomas yelled from the sidelines. Vee smiled at her father. Then she noticed that Mark

Gordon was standing next to him. He grinned at her. She started to smile back, but then remembered about Olivia and the dance. She looked away. Olivia was taking her place on the field. He's probably here to watch her, Vee thought.

Oh, just forget all that, she told herself.

Avery threw the ball down the line and Olivia made a good first touch. She has always been a good dribbler, Vee had to admit. Vee tracked Olivia down the line, calling, "Cross!"

Olivia looked up, saw it was Vee, and didn't make the pass. She kept dribbling and finally lost the ball.

Chris yelled from the sidelines, "Don't hold onto it for so long, Olivia!"

As the game went on, Olivia's selfish play continued. She wouldn't pass. She kept moving too far forward and getting caught offside. Lily and Vee's eyes met. Lily shook her head in disgust. It was obvious Olivia was refusing to pass to Vee and the Bombers needed a goal. Time was running out. They had come so close so many times, but weren't getting their shots off. They were a passing team, and with just one player being selfish, the entire squad was thrown off.

"Bombers, we have got to pass the ball!" Lily called to her teammates, although she was really directing her message to Olivia. The Show Offs were starting to sense that the Bombers were out of sync. They were experienced enough to know that a team that is arguing is a team that is vulnerable.

Molly Barrelton was one of the best players in the league. She got the ball at around the 18 yard line and let loose a screamer. Vee watched as it headed toward the goal. There was no spin on the ball, and that meant that Molly had hit it perfectly. The ball drove toward the goal, heading straight to the upper-right corner. Beth dove to her left, her arms outstretched, her feet off the ground. But she couldn't reach it.

Vee held her breath as the ball arrived. Because of the lack of spin, it flew just an inch too high and clanged against the cross bar with a terrible crash. The pace of the ball was incredible. The goal posts shook, the crowd gasped, and the rebound flew long. The ball bounced back all the way out to the 18-yard line.

Olivia was there. She gathered the ball and looked up to make a pass.

"Send me, Olivia!" Vee called. She could see Olivia's mind working. She knew the last thing she wanted to do was give Vee the ball. Luckily her soccer instincts finally overcame her pettiness and she sent a beautiful through ball to Vee. Vee pounced and headed downfield. She knew the time was now.

The Bombers moved forward as a team and Vee could hear the spectators going crazy on the sidelines.

She beat the two midfielders and then slowed down when she got about 20 yards out. The defenders were trying to slow her down. Vee kept control of the ball, pulling it back and looking for a pass.

"Square!" she heard a voice call. She looked up and saw Olivia was making a perfect run from the back. She wanted Vee to put the ball at her feet, across the face of the goal. With no hesitation, Vee made her pass and timed it perfectly. Without breaking stride, Olivia was able to take a first-time shot. She hit it with her right foot. Well. The ball stayed low and hard and the Show Off goalie had no chance.

The Bombers finally got their goal!

Olivia jumped high in the air, her arms overhead in celebration. All the Bombers came to hug her. The crowd screamed and whistled in appreciation. Vee hung back, but she cheered and clapped with the rest of her team. It was going to take some time for her to get over Olivia's lies, but she would try. Lily would help her. She would follow the Code. She hoped Olivia would too. She would put her team first. Always.

The final whistle blew and the crowds flooded the fields. Tomas gave Vee a tight hug and told her how proud he was of her. The Bombers had secured their first-ever Indoor Championship.

After the game, Olivia approached Vee as she was picking up her ball.

"Nice pass," she said, still glaring at Vee.

"Nice shot," Vee responded, calmly.

Olivia nodded and walked away.

It wasn't great, Vee thought, but it was a start.

LJ ran up behind Vee and jumped on her back like a baby monkey trying to hold onto her mother, "That was awesome!" she yelled. "Oh how I love beating that team."

Vee put Lily down, while still watching Olivia walk away. Lily noticed where she was looking.

"She's a tough one," Lily said.

"I guess I'll be able to play with her," Vee said. "If she doesn't hog the ball."

"Oh, she'll pass, I'll make sure of it," Lily answered. "We all will." Then Lily shook her head, "I still can't believe she's going to the dance with G-4. What a perfect match. Gross."

Vee's head shot up. "What? I thought she asked Mark."

A sly smiled flashed across Lily's face.

"Oh she tried to, but Tabitha ran interference, distracted her, and somehow got her to ask G-4 instead."

"Why did Tabitha do that?" Vee said, trying to hide her glee. Olivia and G-4, what a combination. Tabitha truly was a social genius, Vee thought.

"Oh, no reason," Lily said in a singsong voice and a huge grin.

"What is wrong with you?" Vee asked. "Why are you being such a goof?"

"OOOOh, nooo reason!!!" Lily said again, skipping away.

Vee shook her head. She loved that girl, but sometimes she could really be such a nut. Vee bent down to gather the rest of her things and change her shoes.

"Hey, nice assist," she heard a voice say. She recognized it immediately and broke into a grin. Mark Gordon was standing in front of her.

"Thanks," she said. "How's my hero, Bubba, today?"

"He's a little beat up, but he's tough." Mark answered. Vee noticed that he had a small cut over his eye.

"What happened?" Vee asked, concerned.

"Someone hit me and my helmet cut my face," Mark answered with a shrug. "No biggie."

Vee looked closer. "You really should put some honey on that."

"Honey?" Mark asked with a laugh.

"Yes, it has very good curing properties," Vee said in her most professorial tone.

"Really?"

"Yes, really."

"Good to know," Mark said with a chuckle. "Maybe I'll try it."

Mark and Vee stared at one another for a few seconds, then Vee started to unlace her cleats to change into her boots. No more slipping on the ice for her.

Mark plopped himself down next to Vee on the sideline. "So when you weren't at practice the other night, I was a little worried and came by your dad's restaurant."

"You did?" Vee asked, surprised. Neither Lily nor Tomas had said anything about that.

"I talked to Lily and she told me you had just left."

"Huh," was Vee's only baffled response.

"I guess you worked everything out with your team?" Mark asked.

"Well, sort of. It's not perfect, but for now it's better," Vee answered honestly.

"That's good," Mark said. He started fiddling with his shoes. Vee noticed her father watching their conversation.

"Well, I guess I should get going," Vee said standing up and turning to go.

"Vee?" Mark said.

Vee turned back around, "Please don't tell me I have sticks in my hair again?"

Mark shook his head. "Nope. I wanted to ask you something. Or actually, I want *you* to ask *me* something."

Vee heard rustling behind her. She turned to see Lily and Tabitha and all the Bombers except Olivia standing in a group giggling. Tomas was just off to the right, the same smirk on his face.

Lily started nodding her head up and down. She was holding something behind her back. Tabitha was standing on her toes, clapping her hands together. The two of them looked like they were about to explode with giddiness. Slowly, Lily moved her arms to the front. She was holding a bag. Vee watched as she unzipped it and saw what was inside. She stared at her father. Vee finally began to put it all together.

"We did a little more shopping!" Tabitha and Lily screamed together.

Lily was holding up a hanger. On the hanger was the beautiful butterfly dress. The fabric shimmered, catching the overhead lights like stars on a perfect night. She found her father's eyes. He looked very pleased with himself. Vee grinned and nodded. A feeling of warmth and gratitude filled her soul. She looked at her team. Her friends. Lily. Tabitha. Oh, how she loved her Soccer Sisters, and she knew they loved her.

She turned back to Mark and found him standing close. Directly in front of her. He was smiling, clearly in on it all. He held Bubba out to her, smiled, then asked, "So what do you say, Man U girl, wanna dance?"

Acknowledgments

The Soccer Sisters series would not be possible without the loving support of my husband, Diron Jebejian, and the never-ending patience of my children, Lily and William. I'd also like to thank my brother-in-law Evan Rich for the fantastic cover and Code. I'm grateful to all my family for believing in me always, and specifically to Rosanna Montalbano, for again helping me in getting the Spanish right. Any mistakes are my own.

I am truly indebted to Brandi Chastain, my Official Soccer Sister, for her tireless efforts to promote the sport, empower girls, and inspire generations of fans everywhere. Special thanks also to Dr. Joan Oloff, for her work in educating players, parents and coaches on ACL and other injury prevention. We will keep teaching and Reaching Up, ladies!

Once again, I have to thank Key Biscayne Soccer for the photograph of their U11 Girls Blue team and to Alexandria Fire for helping me create The Soccer Sisters' Code. Thanks to Carey Albertine and Saira Rao at In This Together Media for creating great books about real girls, like Lily and Vee. Thanks to editors Genevieve Gagne-Hawes and Shelley Haley Huntington for all your great comments and insights.

Vee is a fictional character, but was inspired by the indomitable Verenice Merino, who allowed me to use her name and taught me that "tacos" is what cleats are called in Mexico! Thank you, Nana, for everything.

Once again, I want to thank every one of the Yonkers United Rush Roadrunners U9 girls' team, and Yonkers United President Pete Dolgos. Coaching you is one of the joys of my life, and a true privilege.

Finally, I have to thank Stacey Vollman Warwick, for always having my back and being the best friend any one could ever ask for. You define what it means to be a Soccer Sister.

Together Book Clubs: Questions and Activities

1. Why do you think Lily lied to Vee about going to the mall with Tabitha and Olivia? Is it ever okay to lie in order to protect a friend's feelings?

2. In your opinion, would Vee be betraying the Soccer Sisters Code if she were to join Gabriela in starting a new team at her own school? Why or why not?

3. What do you think is the best way for Vee to handle her relationship with Olivia in the future?

4. What makes an object special or meaningful to someone, in the way that Vee's father's car is important to him? What is an object that is special to you and why?

5. Why do you think it is so difficult for Vee to talk to Lily about her problems with Olivia, and about feeling excluded from the soccer sisters?

6. What do you think is the most important rule on the Soccer Sisters' Team Code and why?

7. Why do you think a team doesn't play as well when its members aren't getting along?

8. Why do you think Olivia was so eager to exclude Vee from the team?

9. Vee criticizes "helicopter parents," parents who are too involved with their child's team. How involved do you think parents should be with their child's team?

10. Write your own sisterhood code with your team or group of friends!

About Andrea Montalbano

Andrea Montalbano grew up on a soccer field in Miami. She continued to play through college acting as captain for her Harvard University soccer team and eventually being inducted into the Harvard Varsity Club Hall of Fame.

After college, Andrea pursued a career in journalism, attending Columbia University's Graduate School of Journalism. She was an English anchor at Vatican Radio, and then worked as a writer and Supervising Producer for NBC News and NBC's TODAY program.

Now the mother of two young players, Andrea is coaching, writing, and bringing all her loves together in Soccer Sisters, the follow-up series to Breakaway (Penguin, 2010). Andrea lives outside of New York City with her husband, Diron, and two children.

Discover other titles by Andrea Montalbano:

Soccer Sisters: Lily Out of Bounds

Breakaway

Connect with Andy:

www.andreamontalbano.com

www.facebook.com/soccersisters

Twitter:@andreasoccer

About Brandi Chastain

Brandi Chastain, NCAA, World Cup and Olympics icon, is best known for her game-winning penalty kick against China in the 1999 FIFA Women's World Cup final. She also played on the team that won the inaugural women's World Cup in 1991 and Olympic gold medals in 1996 and 2004. Chastain was an NBC commentator for the 2012 Olympic Games in London.

Brandi is proud to be the official Spokesperson of the Soccer Sisters Series—our Official Soccer Sister!!

Connect with Brandi Chastain:

www.reachupworld.com
www.brandisworld.com
https://www.facebook.com/www.reachup

Twitter: @brandichastain

Other books by In This Together Media:

Mrs. Claus and The School of Christmas Spirit by Rebecca Munsterer

Playing Nice by Rebekah Crane

Personal Statement by Jason Odell Williams

Connect with
In This Together Media:

www.inthistogethermedia.com
https://www.facebook.com/InThisTogetherMedia

Twitter:@intogethermedia